William Stokes

The Olive-Branch

Or, poems on peace, liberty, friendship, & c.

William Stokes

The Olive-Branch
Or, poems on peace, liberty, friendship, & c.

ISBN/EAN: 9783337220006

Printed in Europe, USA, Canada, Australia, Japan

Cover: Foto ©Andreas Hilbeck / pixelio.de

More available books at **www.hansebooks.com**

THE

OLIVE-BRANCH;

OR,

POEMS

ON

PEACE, LIBERTY, FRIENDSHIP, &c.

BY

WILLIAM STOKES,

*Author of a " Prize Essay on War," "A Permanent European
Congress," &c. &c.*

SECOND EDITION, ENLARGED.

Manchester:

THE AUTHOR, 71, ROBERT STREET. C. ON M.

1863.

THE OLIVE-BRANCH

Reviews on the First Edition.

" Here we have poesy of no mean order, dedicated to some of the noblest themes that can thrill the soul of man."—*The Homilist.*

" The poems will be read with pleasure and profit by all who love freedom, and look for the day when wars shall cease."—*Burnley Advertiser.*

" The author of this handsomely got up little volume, is well known as an able writer in the cause of peace.—The poems will be read and appreciated by all who desire the promotion of the happiness of our race."—*The British Friend.*

" We have gone through the work with unfeigned delight. There is a very considerable amount of the true poetic fire burning in its pages."—*Primitive Church Magazine.*

" An elegant volume, containing poetry of a chaste and superior kind."—*Voice of Truth.*

" Both it and its author deserve to be better known."—*Poetical Souvenir.*

" Poetical merits of a very high order."—*Gospel Herald.*

" The author is a genuine follower of the Prince of Peace."—*The Eclectic.*

" Fine thoughts embodied in graceful poetry."—*Rochdale Observer.*

" Contains a variety of poetic and prose pieces, of a first-class order."—*Earthen Vessel.*

" This little volume expresses some noble sentiments, and is characterized throughout by earnest Christian sympathies; it contains also not a little excellent poetry."—*The Freeman.*

" We cordially commend this volume, for its soundness of principle, its earnestness of spirit, as well as its flow and felicity of versification."—*Herald of Peace.*

PREFACE.

It is now more than twenty years since the author of the following pieces became deeply convinced of the incompatibility of war, in any form whatever, with the spirit and precepts of pure Christianity. He was not led to this conviction by " peace publications," for, at that period, it had not been his privilege to read one of them ; nor by the arguments or other influences of any member of the " peace party ;" for he was not then aware of their existence ;—but by an unbiassed perusal of the New Testament alone, and especially those practical portions of it which are intended to regulate the conduct of Christians towards their fellow-creatures at large. He was more particularly impressed with the injunctions, "Recompense to no man evil for evil ;"—" Be not overcome of evil, but overcome evil with good:"—" Love your enemies, do good to them that hate you, and pray for them which despitefully use you and persecute you:"—" If thine enemy hunger, feed him ; if he thirst, give him drink: for in so doing thou shalt heap coals of fire on his head." From that moment to the present day, he has retained the conviction that the *only* contest permissible to the Christian is that of goodness in opposition to evil. This has been his anchor ground for nearly a quarter of a century, and, while acknowledging with gratitude the great additional light which he has received from the masterly arguments employed at the Peace Congresses in Brussels, Paris, Frankfort-on-the-Maine, London and Edinburgh ; and the important information which numerous able works on the peace question have supplied ; yet he must candidly declare, nevertheless, that, in his judgment, there is no ground so solid, no position so safe for the Christian duty of peace with all mankind, as the obligation implied in the Divine injunction to "overcome evil with good."

With "maxims of State" the disciple of Jesus has nothing whatever to do, except so far as they agree with the higher law of his acknowledged Master. These boasted, but equivocal dogmas, are almost invariably "of the earth, earthy." Under the mask of "expediency," "policy," "national honour," "balance of power," &c., they have established a practice which contradicts the Christian religion in a vital particular ; and as these vague doctrines are accepted and quoted as fixed laws, which it is considered to be "unpatriotic," or a "weak sentimentalism," even to question, the national conduct of our entire Christendom has become utterly at variance with the faith which its different nations profess to obey. The consequence of this mistake (not to employ a harsher term) is deplorable beyond all power of description. Instead of aiming to "overcome evil with good," these Christian States studiously, systematically, and by deliberate forethought and design, plan and arrange to *overcome evil with evil.* From the awful contests on the battle-field, down to militias and riflemen, the bent and purpose of the huge military machine are to overcome evil with evil. This is the meaning of every cannon, rifle, blunderbuss and bayonet. This is the sole intention of the "drill," the parade exercise, and military training schools. The one purpose of all this machinery, and the skill with which it is worked, is that of employing evil in overcoming evil with the greatest possible success. Were the Christian injunction so obeyed that to "overcome evil with good" became, as it should be, a law to the nations of Christendom, the war machinery would be an impossibility : hence it is most manifest that the two are incompatible with each other, and contradictory. Consequently, a nation employing a war machinery can never be, so far as this grave particular is concerned, a *Christian* nation at all.

"Whatsoever a man soweth, that shall he also reap," is true on every possible human scale. The indulgence in the "evil" practice of war produces equally evil results in a constantly increasing danger abroad, and heavy taxation and national debt at home. Not to mention the blood-guiltiness which a war policy invariably occasions, and which with a dread certainty entails, sooner or later, national ruin, by provoking Him whose creatures it destroys on every battle-field ;—not to refer to Babylon, Persia, Greece, Rome, and other great States of antiquity, which equally rose and *fell by war*, and whose fate should warn even a Christian England ;—is it not most evident that this policy of "evil" is the cause of every national burden? Civil government, *per se*, is never burdensome. Constituted for "good" by higher than human authority, it has proved itself a blessing to all mankind in every age. Its charges are never oppressive, and produce no discontent ; for it is felt by every intelligent citizen that this sacred institution renders back, in multiplied particulars, a full compensation for whatever outlay its existence may occasion. But not so war. It renders back nothing. It spends life and treasure in its deadly contests, but can return nothing for the awful expenditure. And this is far from being the whole of the injury which it inflicts upon the nations. War, unfortunately, stands not alone and apart, but is dexterously united with the civil government ; and, associating itself with an institution confessedly Divine, it tends to bring upon its associate the danger and ruin which should lie at no door but its own. It has frequently provoked discontent and rebellion among large masses of mankind by its rapacious demands upon national industry ; and the exasperated communities not discriminating between the sword and the sceptre, the soldier and the sovereign,—have confounded the one with the other, and expended their vengeance upon the throne and the monarch, which had been aroused exclusively by the soldier and war. The innocent have thus suffered equally with the guilty, in consequence of an unnatural coalition which should never have been formed at all. And even where the national provocation has not reached this dangerous point, there frequently exists a deep-seated discontent, or a latent restlessness under the heavy burdens imposed upon the State by unproductive armed men, which renders government distasteful to large numbers of the people, and predisposes them to seek relief in political changes of a perilous kind. It is obvious that nations can neither be happy nor safe with the public mind thus constantly chafed, and every friend to constitutional government must feel it to be a serious duty to remove a cause fraught with such imminent danger to the best interests of mankind.

It should not be forgotten, however, that monarchs generally have been far too eager to incur the penalties of war by a gratuitous identity with its crimes and burdens, and that, sooner or later, in one age or another, their criminality has invoked their own punishment. A retributive providence may be slow in constructing its balances, but it is an infallible law, that no nation can indulge in "evil" without reaping in due time the "evil" of its own doings. If any one assurance in Holy Scripture be more solemn and impressive than others, it is the one which comes upon the ear like the knell of death, to warn mankind at large that "God is not mocked."

Slavery is an evil that stands side by side with war,—the twin children of wickedness, whose destiny it is to live, and labour, and perish together. The one attacks the *liberty*, as the other attacks the *life*, of God's vicegerent upon earth. In the slave, man is sold by another; but in the soldier, he sells himself: and just as man is transformed into a beast by the one system, he is equally degraded into a brute by the other. The free action of a noble, independent human being, is forfeited equally in both cases, but with this difference as to the mode—that in the one it is done by compulsion, and in the other with few exceptions, by voluntary barter. They are both alike the degraded offspring of a blind brute force; and the day that witnesses the death of the parent, will also witness the extinction of the soldier and the slave.

To contribute in some humble degree towards this glorious consummation,—this emancipation of mankind from degradation and crime,—is the primary object of the following productions, so far as they relate to slavery and war. The world is almost deluged with publications, both in prose and verse, of an opposite kind, and whole ranks of authors may be seen bending the knee before the popular divinities. Surely one solitary worshipper at another shrine may be pardoned for reminding these devotees of *Mars* and *Pallas* that those rough deities were allowed no place among the sanctities of *Parnassus*, and that it was reserved to a more modern and a more degenerate age to permit the *Muses* to appear upon the battle-field.

"*O limus accipitrem quia semper vivit in armis.*"—Ovid.

Contents.

THE OLIVE-BRANCH.

THE FREEMAN'S SONG.

O GIVE me the freedom to speak as I think,
   And liberty's fulness with Milton to drink;—
To bask on the mountain, or bathe in the stream,
To wander with sages—with poets to dream!

O give me the freedom to utter and teach,
The heart-felt conviction in plain, open speech;
With Cato, and Hampden, and Chatham to stand,
And plead with all boldness the weal of my land!

O give me the freedom to make honest search,
For sect and for party, for creed and for church;—
To act for myself in all matters divine,
Nor "soundings" to take with "another man's line!"

O give me the freedom to stand forth alone,
And vice to expose, though the vice of the throne;
Nor let me be shackled, or fettered, or fined,
When stringing my bow at the faults of mankind!

B

O give me the freedom and home of the brave,
With soil never trod by the foot of the slave;
Where tyrants, and dungeons, and chains are unknown,
And liberty's smile is the stay of the throne!

O give me this treasure!—then perish the gold,
That miser-fools barter for liberty sold!
I'll rove on the mountain, the broad ocean scan,
And sing the lov'd freedom that makes me a man.

A PRAYER FOR UNIVERSAL EMANCIPATION.

"Arise, O God! let not man prevail: O God, lift up thine hand!
to judge the fatherless and the oppressed, that the man of
the earth may no more oppress."—*The Psalms.*

O Thou the Great Almighty!—Power sublime!
    Supreme in glory ere the birth of time,—
Thine awful glance athwart the gloom profound,
Strikes through all nature to her utmost bound;
Surveying men and angels, earth and sky,
Each thought and purpose as they open lie;—
From whom the darkness hides no secret deeds,
Where vice defies thee, or where virtue bleeds;—
Low at thy footstool, Pow'r Divine, I fall,
And Thee adore, great Sovereign Lord of all!

Thou King Eternal! Bliss of Heav'n above!
Whose reign is mercy, and whose throne is love;
Look down with pity, and behold the woe
That mars creation in thy world below;
Where power and pride with infamy unite
To rob the helpless of each holy right,
And Thee defying, make it cause of sin
That man is covered with a darker skin;
And thine own image barter and enchain
As beasts for burden, or as slaves for gain.

For this didst Thou a being give to man ?
Was it for this our common race began ?
Didst Thou to him of paler skin convey
The right his darker brother to betray,
And him from country and from home to steal,
As one too stolid or too base to feel ?
Or didst thou make the paler brother chief,
To act by turns the tyrant and the thief?

No; of "one blood" Thou madest man to be
Equal in honour and in liberty;
Equal the forest and the plains to roam,
To sail the ocean and to choose his home;
Equal to tend the flock or turn the sod,
To serve his country, and obey his God.
In all things equal:—feature, limb and life,
In children's fondness, or in love of wife.
Equal in value as Thy godlike race,
Though rude the language, and though dark the f

Equal in time and all that time has given ;
Equal in death, in judgment, and in heaven.

　Why, then, O Lord, shall guilty man presume
Thy law to cancel in his brother's doom,
And, with insulting impotence, defy
The awful Maker of the earth and sky ?
Shall he Thine image seize as living prey,
And deal defiance in the face of day ?
Shall he degrade his brother to a slave,
And all thy justice and thy wrath outbrave ?
With felon grasp shall he make fast his hold,
Nor loose his victim but for paltry gold?
Shall he thy foe in tyrant pomp abide,
And dare thy vengeance in his brutal pride ?

　O God, appear! lift up thine hand, and smite
The lawless monster, and his boasted might.
He heeds no cry—of wife, or child, or mother,—
Of virgin sister, or of death-doomed brother,—
Of writhing slave, who dies beneath the stroke
Of some sworn foe to every tyrant's yoke,—
Of frenzied husband, maddened to his face,
And doomed to witness to his own disgrace;
Whose raging anguish but provokes the blow
That lays both husband and avenger low.
In vain the groans, the agony, the tears,
For harden'd man no captive brother hears;
But callous-hearted, chuckling o'er his gold,
Brands him a chattel to be bought and sold.

What fell despair, what anguish will he heed,
As father, mother, helpless children, bleed?
What raving parent moves his heart to grief,
As o'er the daughter gloats some sordid thief,
Who counts on beauty as the trading-stock,
To bring more dollars at the auction-block?
    Arise, O Lord, nor let Thy power delay,
But close for ever the oppressor's day;
His pride dash headlong—all his gains o'erthrow,
And lay his falsehood and his triumph low;
Burst every fetter, break each tyrant's chain,
Nor let iniquity for ever reign;
But plead the cause of Afric's injured race,
And brand their spoilers with the world's disgrace.
    Across the deep, where roll Atlantic waves,
Where Freedom boasts her heritage of slaves;
Where Christian doctors prove, with learned pains,
How Christ their Master may be held in chains;
And toil, with midnight study, to unfold
How He, in brethren, may be bought and sold;
O God, arise! their infamy reverse,
Or Freedom's name will be a scorn and curse.
And, ere the slumbering indignation pour
In awful judgment on that blood-stained shore,—
Ere pent-up fires, in flaming billows, sweep
Their bastard freedom to the angry deep,
Give them to make the compensation due—
To "mourn in sackloth, and in ashes" too;

Give them to clear the freeman's soil from shame,
By blotting slavery to the very name;
Give them to act the Christian's noble part—
To love their brother with a brother's heart,
And with him join thy glory to pursue,
Who made them brethren with a different hue.
So come, O God, and let thy will be done,
As in yon heaven, e'en so beneath the sun :
Thus come in glory, thus in mercy reign,
And make our earth a paradise again.

NOTES.

The Church of God a House for Slaves.

The following figures show the number of slaves at the South who are church-members, and the churches they belong to :—

Connected with the Methodist Church South are...	200,000
Methodist, North (in Virginia and Maryland)......	15,000
Missionary and Hard-shell Baptist	175,000
Old-School Presbyterians	12,000
New-School Presbyterians ....supposed	6,000
Cumberland Presbyterians	20,000
Protestant Episcopalians	7,000
Campbellites, or Christian Church	10,000
All other sects combined........................	20,000
Total coloured membership	468,000

Anti-Slavery Standard, Oct. 30, 1858.

At a recent meeting in London, "Miss Remond said, ' It may not be inappropriate on my part, as the representative of THREE MILLIONS AND A HALF OF SLAVES IN THE UNITED STATES, who cannot speak for themselves, to say—I thank you.'"

INVOCATION TO THE SPIRIT OF PEACE.

COME over the mountain, come over the sea,
Thou First-born of heaven, thou Pride of the free !
Come fresh on the morning, with wings of the dove,
And strew in thy passage the blessings of love.

Appear in thy radiance, thou Angel of light,
And chase from creation the gloom of the night ;
Disperse the thick shadows that over us spread,
And be to all nations as life from the dead.

Drive back to their caverns the dark hosts of death,
And scatter the forces of war with thy breath ;
Proclaim to the world a new era begun,
And let it be lasting as light from the sun.

In broad open day shew the scroll of the dead,
And let it by heroes and monarchs be read ;
And give them to blush for the guilt of the hour,
That made war and bloodshed the "balance of power."

Array to their vision the souls of the slain,
With heart-broken widows and orphans in train :
Tear off the disguise from their " glory" and pride,
And ask what they shew for the men who have died ?

Before them display, in its ruin and fire,
Some Kertch or Canton, with the woe of the sire ;
Then, pointing to wealth spent in battle and flame,
Demand what they give in return—but a name.

Proclaim that the Judge of the quick and the dead
Will " make inquisition for blood" they have shed ;
Yet turn far away heavy judgments in store,
If, mourning their folly, they " learn war no more."

Thus come, gentle Peace, fix thy reign upon earth,
And bring the glad day of the world's second birth :
"The bow in the cloud," when dark thunder-storms cease,
Be thou to creation, sweet Spirit of Peace.

TRUE FREEDOM.

ADDRESSED TO LOUIS KOSSUTH.

" Wisdom is better than weapons of war :" *Holy Scripture ;*
Eccles. ix. 18.

HAIL, patriot chief ! whose flowing themes
Roll eloquent like golden streams,

Through Saxon crowds who throng to learn
Thy "thoughts that breathe and words that burn ;"
Who joyously renew their youth,
While echoing back thy mighty truth ;
Hail to thee, chief! now nobly free,
And hail, Hungarian liberty!

Yet Chieftain, start not when the Muse,
The hist'ry of the past reviews,
To show that fields of blood impart
Nor life nor joy to freedom's heart.
The " olden time," the " days of yore,"
When saint and savage sank in gore,
Proclaim, who trusts to warlike deed,
Trusts freedom to a broken reed.

Of old, thy loved Pannonian plain
Groan'd loud beneath the warrior's train.
The Roman there with brow severe,
The savage Hun without a tear,
The Goth who knew no law but hate,
And Longobard with pride elate ;
These doom'd thy Fatherland to groan,
As groan all lands where war is known.

Thy Magyar father, fierce and light,
Then came like roe o'er Carpath's height.
A freeman's home great Arpad sought,
For freeman's home the conqueror fought.

He fought and gained the freeman's prize,
Yet bade no native slave arise ;
But proved how *Freedom's warlike reign*
Can forge the tyrant's iron chain.

Full oft since then the battle's surge
Has been the Magyar's boast and scourge ;
Full oft beneath the sword he hired,
Has Magyar liberty expired.
While Moslem, Russ, and Hapsburg proud
Have each in turn proclaimed aloud,
While pointing to the patriot's chain—
In Freedom's cause the sword is vain.

Then Magyar chief,—thou patriot, say,
Shall blood again disgrace the day,
When Freedom, rising in her might,
Compels the despot's power to flight ?
Is there no weapon but the spear,
To fill his tyrant heart with fear ?
None brave but he in coated mail,
To make his coward hirelings quail ?

Has Truth no strength, and Faith no power,
To aid in Freedom's struggling hour ?
Or will High Heaven forget to plead,
When despots vaunt and nations bleed ?
Or shall the *Patriot's* hope afford
No confidence but in the sword,

And rally or decline in turn,
As slaughter spreads and cities burn ?

Oh Kossuth ! while thy tongue of might
Provokes great nations to the fight,
That Raab's flood and Danube's shore
Would crimson dye with human gore ;—
Think how thy words of magic power
Might nerve them for the coming hour,
When Truth alone shall deal the blow,
To lay each " proud oppressor low."

Thou honoured man ! a fairer fame
Awaits to crown thy noble name,
Than battle-field or bloody fray
E'er gave—or e'er can take away.
But mark,—the highest tide will ebb,
And man, not fate, weaves his own web ;
Weave thou thy web, strike out at flood,
And show thy flag unstained with blood.

Creation waits this master mind,
Who to the vulgar " glory" blind,
Will venture, armed *with truth alone*,
To dash for aye the tyrant's throne.
The post is open ; Chieftain, say,
Art thou unequal to the day ?
Or, strong in more than mortal grace,
SHALL KOSSUTH FILL THIS VACANT PLACE ?

APPEAL OF THE AFRICAN SLAVE TO BRITISH SYMPATHY.

FAR on the mountain,
    Across the blue sea,
Where springs the pure fountain
    In dark Abomey;
Where Nile rolls his waters
    Through desert and plain,
And Africa's daughters
    Wear slavery's chain:

They cry in strange voices
    To Britain's fair isles,
Where Freedom rejoices
    And Liberty smiles;—
" O ye who *can* sever
    The bands of the slave,
Whose shores have been ever
    The home of the brave;

" Whose stern tones of thunder
    All tyrannies shake,
Whose *word* snaps asunder
    The fetters they make;

O once more awaken
  Your work to complete,
And let the forsaken
  Be heard at your feet.

" The white man yet tears us
  From homes that are free;
His death-ship yet bears us
  Across the wide sea:
But happy the mother
  Who *there* finds a grave,
And sister and brother
  Whose tomb is the wave.

" Of ' one blood ' they tell us
  We all have been made,
Then brutally sell us
  As ' chattels ' in trade :
With no spark of pity
  For woes all untold,
In Liberty's city*
  We're barter'd for gold.

" O save us !   O save us
  From deeds of the ' free !'
From men who enslave us,
  Then shout ' Liberty !'

---

* Washington, United States.

From fiends who take measure
    Of muscle and bone,
Then reckon their treasure
    In limbs like their own.

" By all that is tender
    In womanly grace;
By all that should render
    To woman her place;
By rights that are given
    To all from on high,
As sacred as heaven,
    As pure as the sky;

" By wrongs of the friendless,
    The groans of the weak,—
The tears that flow endless
    Down Africa's cheek;
By blood of the slaughtered
    That cries from her sands,
By shrieks of the tortured
    In merciless bands;

" By woman now raving
    In agonies wild,
And fierce for the saving
    Her *last* lovely child;

By Him who will render
  To all men their deeds,
Who proves the Defender
  When innocence bleeds;

" O Britons, arouse you!
  Your strong help we crave;
And once more espouse you
  The cause of the slave.
Or shall we, unheeded,
  Sink under the chain?
And all we have pleaded
  Be pleaded in vain?"

No, never! No, never!
  Let Britons reply;
For Freedom, as ever,
  WE'LL WORK TILL WE DIE.
Your cause we will cherish
  The universe o'er,
Till tyrannies perish,
  AND SLAVES ARE NO MORE.

THE ATLANTIC TELEGRAPH CABLE.

*(Respectfully inscribed to the Directors of the Atlantic Telegraph
Company, by whom the following noble message was transmitted
to America through the medium of that chief of modern miracles,
as its appropriate consecration to the union of mankind : " Europe
and America are united by Telegraph. Glory to God in the
highest ; peace on earth, and goodwill towards men."—AUGUST
16, 1858.)*

WHAT " still small voice," what gentle breath of heaven,
   Moves noiseless through the deep from shore to shore?
What sound prophetic, from blue ocean given,
   Heralds an age unknown in days of yore ?

It tells of glory—of that " highest glory,"
   On earth unsung by every victor host;
It bears no tale of battle, red and gory,
   To spread alarm on some far distant coast.

In sweeter strains—in tones of holy greeting,
   With no boom'd cannon dark'ning nature's sun,
It sings of " Peace on earth," and joyous meeting,
   Of kingly hands and queenly hearts made one.

In notes divine, borne silent through the waters,
   It sings—" Goodwill to man " the earth around,
And bids both worlds for aye forego their slaughters,
   Spreading despair and death on all the ground.

In wedlock bands it joins two mighty nations,
    Bidding them pledge their troth in weal or woe;
Strikes the sweet chord for coming generations,
    And pours heaven's music on the world below.

Whence came the sound? And whence that song supernal?
    Whence the new language wing'd from shore to shore?
Not from some battle-field, dark, foul, infernal,
    Where Death rides horrid on a sea of gore.

From scenes of blood, where brother strives with brother.
    And each alike grasps at his brother's life,
Where men as fiends all kindly feelings smother,
    And blanch humanity in deadly strife—

There comes no sound of aught but hellish raging,
    Loud, fiery curses from expiring breath;
Where furious hosts, more furious conflict waging,
    Plunge down their thousands to an endless death.

Not thence comes friendship, or goodwill to nations,
    Not thence the *coil* that forms "the bond of peace;"
But where meek Commerce breathes warm aspirations,
    For the bright day when murd'rous War shall cease.*

---

* The following is the copy of a complimentary message from the Directors of the New York, Newfoundland, and London Telegraph Company, in reply to the above message transmitted to them from the Directors of the Atlantic Telegraph Company.

C

Or where, enthroned amidst true hearts and loyal,
    Great England's Queen holds friendship through the
With distant Ruler, who, in all things royal,   [deep
    Cares but the substance, not the name, to keep.

Not empty words are these, nor courtly phrases,
    Warm to the ear, but cold and false at heart;
From pledge of nations, heard with world-wide praises,
    Both Queen and Ruler never more may part.*

"New York, August 18.—The Directors of the New York, Newfoundland, and London Telegraph Company, desire to express to the Directors of the Atlantic and London Telegraph Company, their joy and gratitude for the facilities and privileges of coming into closer union and fellowship with them and their fellow-men throughout the world. May the success that has crowned our labours secure to the nations of the earth a perpetual bond of peace and friendship."

* The following are copies of the messages exchanged between Her Majesty the Queen of Great Britain, and the President of the United States of America :—

"THE QUEEN TO THE PRESIDENT.

"The Queen desires to congratulate the President upon the successful completion of this great international work, in which the Queen has taken the deepest interest.

"The Queen is convinced that the President will join her in fervently hoping that the electric cable, which now connects Great Britain with the United States, will prove an additional link between the two nations, whose friendship is founded upon their common interests and reciprocal esteem.

Whence came the sound?   Beneath the ruffled ocean
The merchant princes joyous greetings send;
And civic magnates learn, with fond emotion,
To sink distinctions in the name of friend.*

" The Queen has much pleasure in thus directly communicating
with the President, and in renewing to him her best wishes for
the prosperity of the United States."

"THE PRESIDENT TO THE QUEEN.

"The President cordially reciprocates the congratulations of
Her Majesty the Queen on the success of the great international
enterprise, accomplished by the skill, science, and indomitable
energy of the two countries.

"It is a triumph more glorious, because far more useful to
mankind, than was ever won by conqueror on the field of battle.
May the Atlantic Telegraph, under the blessing of Heaven, prove
to be a bond of perpetual peace and friendship between the kindred nations, and an instrument destined by Divine Providence
to diffuse religion, civilization, liberty, and law throughout the
world.

"In this view will not all the nations of Christendom sponta-
neously unite in the declaration that it shall be for ever neutral,
and that its communications shall be held sacred in passing to
the places of their destination, even in the midst of hostilities?
                    (Signed)   "JAMES BUCHANAN."

* "TO THE RIGHT HON. SIR WALTER CARDEN,
         LORD MAYOR, LONDON.

" New York, August 21, 1858.—I congratulate your Lordship
on the successful laying of the Atlantic cable, uniting the conti-
nents of Europe and America; the cities of London and New
York; Great Britain and the United States.   It is a triumph of

O sacred Science! Commerce stands thy debtor,
  Waiting thy guidance to a nobler day;
Then bind the globe in one *electric* fetter,
  And o'er the universe exert thy sway.

The world unites! All hail! around creation,
  Carry the news through lands enslaved or free;
Spread the glad tidings o'er each jarring nation,
  And loud proclaim that men will brothers be.

---

science and energy over time and space, uniting more closely the bonds of peace and commercial prosperity; introducing an era in the world's history, pregnant with results beyond the conception of a finite mind. To God be the praise !

(Signed)   "DANIEL G. TIEMAN, Mayor."

The Lord Mayor, immediately upon receiving the message, sent the following reply :—

"TO THE HON. DANIEL G. TIEMAN, MAYOR OF NEW YORK.

"The Lord Mayor of London most cordially reciprocates the congratulations of the Mayor of New York upon the success of so important an undertaking as the completion of the Atlantic Telegraph Cable. It is indeed one of the most glorious triumphs of the age, and reflects the highest credit upon the energy, skill, and perseverance of all parties entrusted with so difficult a duty; and the Lord Mayor sincerely trusts that, by the blessing of Almighty God, it may be the means of cementing those kindly feelings which now exist between the two countries.—23rd Aug., 1858."

" Pay out," "pay out," the golden-threaded cable ;
" Pay out " the cord that binds the world in one :
Tell sallow Asia and the Afric sable,
    That heav'n-born freedom is for them begun.

Britain ! stand faithful to thy high vocation,
    Write " Peace on earth " on each historic page ;
Uncoil thy bond to every distant nation,
    And make Victoria's reign the Golden Age.

BETTER DAYS DESIRED.

'Tis not for the days of the hero I sigh,
    When kings lived for battle and panted to die ;
When war was the watchword of brave men and proud,
And bloodshed the glory and boast of the crowd.

No sigh do I breathe for the tyrant who sway'd,
His rude iron sceptre o'er slaves he had made ;
Who fawned at his footstool, and called him their Lord,
Yet lived but to sever the rule they abhorr'd.

Nor yet do I sigh for the days when there dwelt,
A darkness o'er nations like that which was " felt,"
When Egypt was ruin'd ;—a " sackcloth of hair,"
By priestly hands woven and spread abroad there.

For these days of darkness, come Virtue, and weep
O'er nations in fetters and Freedom asleep ;
A world rank with poison, or teeming and foul,
With vipers that hiss, and with tigers that howl.

I sigh for the days when the tyrant shall fall,
When slaves sycophantic no more heed his call ;
When earth shall resound with the song of the free,
And men with their fellow-men brothers shall be.

I sigh for the days when the hero in arms,
No longer shall fill the wide world with alarms ;
When spears but as " pruning-hooks " glisten in store,
When swords become " plough-shares," AND WAR BE NO
    MORE.

I sigh for the age when religion shall be,
No bye-word for party, nor hypocrite's fee ;
But when, breathing o'er us sweet grace from above,
Her blessings shall prove her the best gift of love.

Roll on, then, ye spheres, and add swiftness to time,
Nor long let the world wait for scenes so sublime ;
But if we behold not these treasures in store,
We'll hail them when " cast in their shadows before."

Roll on, ye slow ages, that He may appear,
Whose coming shall " scatter " armed hosts with his fear ;
Who, true to his promise, for freedom will plead,
And crush in his anger both " Serpent " and " seed."

THE EASTERN QUESTION.

"THE Crescent* wanes,"—the Eaglet† flies,
   And flaps his wing in Eastern skies.
The Lion‡ prowls along the shore,
And vents his rage in smothered roar;
While chasing clouds in angry form,
Herald the bursting of the storm.

The distant thunders fiercely roll,
And shake from "centre to the pole."
The Northern Bear,§ intent on prey,
Surveys the tempest with dismay—
Defies the storm he fears to meet,
Then turns him to his dark retreat.

In that retreat the rugged beast,
Can see no evil in a feast.
If tempted out by human gore,
He treads a path long trod before.
The way is old, and old the work,
That swallows Chinaman or Turk.

---

* The national emblem of Turkey.
†   Ditto   of France.
‡   Ditto   of England.
§ The assumed Ditto   of Russia.

That Eagle circling now so gay,
Suck'd Roman blood a live-long day ;
And spread on Algiers' sands a brood,
That made a turban'd host their food.
The carcase slain, they take their fill,
And prove their nature Eagle still.

That roaring Lion, King of Beasts,
Makes lordly meals at human feasts.
The weak Hindoo, the Affghan brave,
The Caffre, and the Burman slave,
The Dyak, Scind, and China fair,
Proclaim who takes " the Lion's share."

But these are Lords,—and must they starve,
While Bruin claims his turn to carve ?
Shall they vacate the royal seat,
And see him all the ' Turkey' eat ?
No, never ! or he'll learn to play,
Their fav'rite game some other day.

Feast on, right Royal " Diners out,"
Drive back the Bear with furious shout ;
Feast quickly on, make short the work,
For light is breaking on the Turk.
At his own board he'll take his place,
Nor wait the Christian " saying grace."

Nor he alone, but other prey,
Waits on the wing for coming day.
A calmer morn is rising fast;
Haste ! or the feast will be your last.
One other storm, *one* struggle o'er,
And man shall be your food no more.

WAR IN THE CRIMEA AND THE SEA OF AZOFF.

AND this is progress ! this the growth of nations !
  The royal training for an empty name !
The model deed for future generations,
  To lure them on to " glory" and to fame !

This the proud work of *Christian* might and treasure !
  The boon of mercy to a world depress'd !
The sacred pledge, that without stint or measure,
  Some future age with freedom shall be blest !

For this the Saxon and the Frank united,
  Make common cause with Infidel profane !
For freedom's sake, the Cross and Crescent plighted,
  Pour seas of blood along the Russian plain !

Oh, vile delusion ! Can the reign of terror,
  Confer true freedom on a race depraved ?
Can fields of blood redeem mankind from error ?
  Or burst the fetters of a land enslaved ?

Will broken hearts, and widows' loud bewailing,
  With twice ten thousand orphans' piercing cries,
Show the proud cause of liberty prevailing ?
  Or give to serfdom aught that freemen prize ?

Can slaughtered hosts, with miles of martial thunder,
  The iron tempest, and the cannon's roar ;
The burning homestead, or the wholesale plunder,
  That robs the widow of her scanty store ;—

E'er prove to men how freedom is progressing,
  Or drive the Despot from his slavish work ?—
Can lust and theft convey a freeman's blessing,
  Or teach a holier faith to serf or Turk ?

Britain, go weep that deeds thus vile and savage,
  Are done by freemen in the Christian name !
Go mourn in sackcloth that thy warriors ravage,
  The peasant's home, nor " blush to call it fame !"

List to the cries to yonder Heavens ascending,
  The widow's wail, the orphan's heavy groan ;
Then at the feet of heaven's Avenger bending,
  Ask,—*How shall Britain for this guilt atone ?*

NOTES.

" *The Turkish troops were very busy pillaging the dead; an occupation which most of us were employed in, more or less.* I did not, however, come across any sables in my explorations. *We, however, shall have grand " looting" at Sebastopol, when my China experience may avail me.* This is a horrible way to talk, and no doubt will shock you much ; but it is one of the concomitants of grim war, and perhaps one of the most agreeable."—*From a Medical Officer in the Crimean War.*

" As we approach the towns and villages, the inhabitants desert them, and as soon as we come to halt our men disperse through them in search of plunder, and such a scene you could not imagine as is to be seen here in a few minutes. Thousands of men loaded with tables, chairs, sofas, chests of drawers, pier glasses, geese, ducks, cabbages, fowls,—in fact, everything that can be imagined. Our men lie on beautiful beds and costly sofas in the open air."—*Do.*

"——— At Yenikale, not only did the garrison retire, but the inhabitants also,—terrible tidings of rapacity and violence had reached them. Their fears were well founded, for very soon their own town was plundered of everything moveable, *and the ships of war were receptacles for the plundered property.*"—*History of the War against Russia, vol.* 2, *p.* 332.

" It is to be regretted that the French general in command of the place allowed the soldiers to plunder not only the houses, but the persons of the inhabitants."—*Do.*, p. 332.

Berdiansk.—" All government property was destroyed,—*this included corn to the value of £*50,000.—*Do.*, p. 340.

Genitschi.—" The stores and corn (destroyed) were at least worth £150,000."—*Do.*, p. 341.

Taganrog.—" When we arrived at Taganrog, we vented our spite upon the Russians. As for my part, I burned everything I could—in fact, anything that would catch fire, I committed to the flames."—*Do.*, 388.

Gheisk.—" However, we burned all his stock, consisting of 574 large stacks of corn, besides his granaries and everything that belonged to him ; his corn alone was valued at £30,000."—

"We are still cruising about the sea, burning and destroying everything, besides what we take away. We live like fighting cocks."—"You may depend when I come across any money, I know I can find a place for it; but it is very scarce."—"We have in all taken fifteen vessels, burned twelve, and sent two to be sold at Constantinople, and sent one away with the Russian prisoners on board, fifty-seven in number, *without compass or anything to steer by, to find the best of their way wherever chance would let them go.*"—*Do.*, p. 388.

Can anything be conceived more diabolical, more fiendish than this? To send away a vessel with fifty-seven prisoners without the means necessary for their preservation! And this by Englishmen,—and in the pay of a *Christian* people! If it be true, (and who can question it?) "be sure your sin will find you out," what may not be expected as a punishment? Oh War, thou art a thief, a robber and a scoundrel, all the world over!

Some of the atrocities at Kertch by our "Allies" the Turks, and others, I should be ashamed to mention.—W. S.

THE ANGEL OF PEACE.

RING, ring the sweet bells, and unfurl the gay banners!
 Let cold party-feeling and enmity cease;
Arise, ye glad nations, with lofty hosannahs!
 And welcome with triumph the angel of peace.

Long, long have the foemen dealt fury around them;
 Too long spread the flame of destruction and death;
Too long has the demon of discord spell-bound them,
 And blasted the hope of the world with his breath.

Sing, sing the loud chorus! his spell is now broken,
   And nations once more breathe the air of the free ;
His watchword of "glory" shall henceforth be spoken,
   To die with the echo that floats on the sea.

For, dove-like, the angel has passed o'er the waters,
   And wept when he saw but a deluge of blood ;
His olive-branch waved o'er the scene of the slaughters,
   And Peace spread her "bow" on the face of the flood.

Then sing! for the ark safely rests on the mountain,
   The crimson-dyed waters haste, blushing, away ;
The sun gilds afresh both the stream and the fountain,
   And man hails with rapture the the smile of the day.

Then join the loud chorus! unfurl the gay banners!
   Let peace be the watchword the universe o'er ;
Unite, all ye nations, in lofty hosannahs!
   And sing, " Peace our glory!" and " Peace evermore!"

AMERICAN SLAVERY.

"Weep with them that weep."— PAUL.

WHAT sounds of woe come floating o'er the ocean,
   Like the death-groanings of some tortured slave ?
What cries are heard above the wild commotion
   Of tempests thundering to the foaming wave ?

Are they the moanings of the fettered nations,
  Whose blood-bought freedom kings now hold in thrall;
Whose stricken sons, through gloomy generations,
  Live but to mourn their noble country's fall?

Or come the cries from serfs of toil and sorrow,
  As cattle deemed for some proud noble's gain;
Whose blank despair not even hope can borrow,
  From future bursting of the tyrant's chain?

Ah, no! from realms besotted or benighted,
  By kingly misrule, or by noble's pride,
Such wailing comes not; though with prospects blighted,
  Whole nations weep o'er liberty denied.

In Europe's darkest, guiltiest recesses,
  Siberia's horrors, or a Poland's throes,
Where Czar or Hapsburg freedom's right suppresses,
  And flings back insult on a people's woes;—

No cry is heard on Heaven so loudly calling,
  For vengeance on the robber and the knave,
Nor deed so dark, so cruel or appalling,
  Inflicted on the unbefriended slave,—

As floats across the wide Atlantic billow,—
  As done where Freedom boasts her loved abode;
Where rests the head each on a freeman's pillow,
  And Christian truth directs the way to God.

There Freedom's self, all kingly tyrants spurning,
  Becomes a tyrant far more fierce than they;
Each human right, each tender claim upturning,
  And Heaven defying in the face of day.

Religion there, once guide and light to reason,
  Its manly virtues aiding to unfold,
Shakes hands with Mammon, and proclaims the treason,
  That man may sell his fellow-man for gold.

Oh, lost to honour!—dead to holy feeling!
  Pious in crime, and prayerful but to sin!
In words most saintly, while in black arts dealing,
  Like painted "sepulchres," all foul within.

Cease, cease the cry of Freedom and her mission;
  Earth sickens at the dark imposture there,
And spurns the vile and hellish imposition,
  Though aped with all the mockery of prayer.

Go, heal the woes of yonder Negro brother;
  Go, give him back the partner of his life;
Restore her infant to the raving mother,
  Nor snap again the bond of man and wife.

Close up the market, nor insult creation,
  By selling woman as the hireling's slave;
Blot from your deeds the thrice-curs'd profanation,
  And let the world for once pronounce you brave.

Till then, stand off,—wide as the poles asunder,
Nor dare the vengeance of the blackening sky ;
Insulted Heaven speaks in the rolling thunder—
"WHO STEALS OR SELLS HIS BROTHER-MAN SHALL DIE."[*]

NOTES.

"I preached in a Campbellite Baptist chapel, in Lewis county, on the sinfulness of slavery. Eight of the two hundred members are slaveholders. One sold a slave to the slave-traders the day he became a member. Another member was a slave-driver and a preacher of a pro-slavery gospel. At Mayslick, a Baptist minister owned three slaves, a mother and her two daughters. He sold the daughters. One of them was in prison when I was there, about to be sent to the far south. The mother was almost broken-hearted. She was a member of the same church as her master, and the church could see no wrong in the sale. At Frankfort there is a coloured Baptist church ; three hundred are slaves ; sixty are free ; the pastor is a slave. Mr. Wilkinson, a Baptist minister for whom I preached, is also a slave ; he is buying himself, but will be compelled by law to leave the State when free. His wife and children are slaves. He looked sad as he told me this."—*Rev. E. Mathews.*

"A fugitive slave, named Tom Wilson, aged forty-five, recently arrived in Liverpool from New Orleans, stowed away in the hold of the cotton ship, 'Metropolis.' He was slave-born, and, amongst his sufferings, *was sold away from his wife and three children.*"

WOMEN TO BE RAFFLED FOR AND SOLD.—Selected from recent advertisements.—"Opportunity of obtaining a waiting-woman

---

[*] Exodus xxi. 16.

for 1s. To be raffled for, a waiting-woman, with a child eight years of age, and other subjects of value. Tickets may be had at No. 91, rua do Roseria." "To be sold, a little mulatto, two years of age, very pretty, and well adapted for a festival present (Christmas box). No. 3, rua dos Latoeris." "To be sold, a wet nurse mulatto girl, aged twenty; has very good milk, her first child now four months old. Rue da St. Pedre, No 180." "To be sold—a black woman, five months gone with child, fit for all kinds of service. Largo de Poco, No. 5." "To be sold, a waiting woman with milk, and with a son eight months old. She may be had either with or without child, has the qualifications of a good waiting woman, and is without vice of any kind."

THE MODERN DRUID.

(Written at " Stonehenge" on Salisbury Plain.)

In days of yore the Druid sage,
　Assembled here his clan ;
And from the dark and mystic page,
　Spoke war and woe to man.

Or in this roofless, sacred fane,
　With horrid Moloch rites,
Pour'd blessings on each lawless train,
　That led their savage fights.

He told of war, and vengeance dire,
　To every conquered foe ;
He doom'd the captive wretch to fire,
　And bade the embers glow.

D

But *now* no more the frantic dance,
　Nor cruel Moloch glare;
No warrior comes to break his lance,
　No Druid to his prayer.

No more the human victim bleeds,
　The living for the dead;
No more are seen the Druid deeds,
　Nor heard the Druid's tread.

A nobler race now hold the land
　Who boast a nobler law;
No more a Druid leads his band
　To desolating war.

Save where on yonder distant plain,
　With banners floating round;
Gay sterried hosts march to the strain
　Of music's martial sound.

There stands the priest, in solemn guise,
　(No *Druid's* name he bears,)
To heaven he turns uplifted eyes,
　And pours to heaven his prayers.

" O God of Mercy, God of Love,
　To whom we owe our breath,
Send down thy grace from heaven above,
　And bless the work of Death.

" Go forth, O God, with these to war,
  In battle give them skill ;
Write in their hearts the manly law,
  And teach them how to kill."

Oh, sacred pile ! this pagan prayer,
  Inspires a solemn dread ;
For all its warlike cries declare,
  " THE DRUID IS NOT DEAD."*

---

* On the last day of the year 1843, the ceremony of consecrating the colours of the 44th regiment was performed by the
" venerable Archdeacon" Wilberforce. It was on that occasion
that he offered the prayer referred to in the above lines. The
following are extracts from that prayer, from which it is evident
beyond all question that

            " THE DRUID IS NOT DEAD."

" O Lord God of Hosts, who art God of the armies of heaven,
and amongst the inhabitants of earth, look down, we beseech
thee, upon us, thy unworthy servants, who come before thee in
the name of Jesus Christ our Lord, and extend to us thy accus-
tomed favour and protection. Bless, O Lord, this day, the
work of our hands ; yea, prosper thou our handy-work. Hear
us, as thou art wont ; hear us, O Lord, as thou didst hear thy
people of Israel in the old time ; be thou with us as thou wast
with Joshua upon the plains of Jericho, and by the waters of
Merom......be thou in the midst of our hosts as thou wast on
the plains with these thy servants at Badajos and Waterloo.
Grant that these banners, committed this day to these brave
men, thy servants, may ever be maintained by courageous
hearts, and held up by arms of strength ; cover thou the heads
of their defenders in the day of battle. Be thou their buckler
and the strength of their armour," &c. &c.

On this equivocal service of a minister of the Prince of Peace, the *Voluntary* commented in the following severe but appropriate terms.

"We have seen with pain and regret, the venerated name of Wilberforce connected with what we must be allowed to designate the blasphemous and barbarous ceremony of consecrating regimental colours. On the conformity, or otherwise, of such proceedings of canonical rule, we will leave learned ecclesiastics to decide; but we do not hesitate to denounce the practice as to the last degree anti-Christian and heathenish. When it was sought to interest the late William Wilberforce in the struggles of the Greeks for liberty and independence, he frankly declared that his principles as a Christian and a man of peace, would not permit him to render aid in furnishing them with the munitions of war, although to enable them to release themselves from the intolerable burden of a foreign yoke. That distinguished philanthropist, much as he sympathised with all that were oppressed, was too conscientious to manifest his compassion at the expense of his principles. He, therefore, restricted the proofs of his philo-hellenism to offering to subscribe to the healing of the sick and wounded, thus aiding to mitigate the miseries attendant upon those warlike operations which he would not seem to countenance. We may, therefore, easily conceive with how little complacency the spirit of the father would regard the conduct of the son, supposing him to be conscious of his proceedings. If we remember aright, the occasion which gives rise to these remarks is either the third or the fourth on which Archdeacon Wilberforce, of Surrey, has exhibited as a consecrator of military ensigns. If the religion of Christ forbade the father, a private member of the church, to countenance a band of patriots in warlike resistance to their invaders and oppressors, how much more criminal must it be in his son, a dignified clergyman, to use his ecclesiastical authority for the purpose of giving, or pretending to give, the sanction of the Prince of Peace to war, as a profession?"

A PARAPHRASE OF PSALM CXLVI.

WHILE I have breath, that breath shall be,
  For ever spent in praising thee,
  My Father, God, and Friend :
Thy praise shall be my fresh delight,
In youth, in age, by day, by night,
  Till mortal life shall end.

Put not your trust in earthly kings,—
Those dazzling shadows, fleeting things,
  That perish in a day ;
Nor in the son of man confide,
Whose pomp, and power, and thoughts of pride,
  Fade, like a dream, away.

Thrice happy he, and he alone,
Who makes the great Jehovah's throne,
  His refuge and his trust ;—
Whose confidence unchanged shall be,
In Jacob's God, while mortals flee,
  To perish in the dust.

He, the great Lord of heaven and earth,
Gave to the vast creation birth,
  And filled the mighty deep ;
His truth he keeps from age to age,
But clothes with shame th' oppressor's rage,
  When helpless sufferers weep.

The hungry poor, Jehovah feeds,
The prisoner's chain he breaks, and pleads
　　His cause against the proud ;
With sight restored he'll bless the blind,
And raise to joy each humble mind,
　　With heavy sorrow bowed.

On righteous souls his love shall rest ;—
The orphan and the widow, prest
　　With grief, he'll ne'er despise ;
He'll turn the wicked upside down,
And scatter with his vengeful frown
　　Their vanity and lies.

Then, Zion, pour thy lofty praise,
And the loud song of triumph raise,
　　To God—thy God—and King :
He thy great Saviour, ever reigns;
Then sing, in everlasting strains,—
　　His endless glory sing.

HEAVEN DESIRED.

Rise, my soul, and soar on high,—
　　Rise to joys above the sky;
Spread thy wings, thy fetters break,
Low-born earthly joys forsake.

There th' Eternal Father reigns,
O'er the bright celestial plains ;
There from mercy's boundless stores,
Bliss unspeakable he pours.

There the Son, with glory crown'd,
Sheds benignant smiles around ;
And invites to sweet repose,
On the breast that bare our woes.

There the Spirit, breathing peace,
Bids our care for ever cease ;
And inspires the golden strains
Heard but on those blissful plains.

There th' angelic hosts adore
Him who all our sorrows bore ;
While their thronging ranks proclaim
Endless honour on his name.

There the church, Immanuel's bride,*
Sits exalted at his side ;
Sharing with her Lord the throne,†
Won by love to her alone.

---

* Rev. xix. 7—9, and xxi. 9.
† Rev. iii. 21, and 2 Tim. ii 12.

There the Spring for ever glows,
There the life-stream ever flows;
There the day, for ever bright,
Rolls in joy with "no more night."

There no Summer's heated breath,
Spreads, unseen, a venom'd death;
Nor a tear in sorrow's eye
Mars the beauty of the sky.

Rise, then, soul; from earth arise,
Wing thy way to yonder skies;
Longer here why would'st thou stay?
Haste thee, spirit, haste away.

A REMONSTRANCE, &c.

(Addressed to Charles Mackay, on reading his poem on the Battle of Inkerman.)

Alas! alas! the poet sings
    Of war, and camps, and jarring kings;
Of deeds that crimson Alma's flood,
And foul an Inkerman with blood;
Of slaughtered hosts, of murd'rous strife,
And "glory" quaff'd from human life.

Alas ! that he who nobler themes,
So sweetly mingled with his dreams ;
Who sang the "good time coming,"—when,
Men shall be nothing less than men ;
When strife, and blood, and war shall flee
Far from the dwellings of the free :—
Alas ! that he should bend the wing,
And stoop of deadly War to sing ;
That rage and blood, his muse should fire,
And murder tune his gentle lyre ;
That harp so sweet forgot to moan,
Where heav'n, and earth, and nature groan ;
But struck forth honour to the deed,
That makes ten thousand widows bleed.

Was there no higher range for song ?
No fitter theme to bear along
The music of the bard, who gave
Hope to the cabins of the slave,—
Who sounded in melodious strain
How man depressed shall soar again,
And every sacred right assume,
As life recovered from the tomb ?—
Was there no tender, gentler theme,
To guide the sweet poetic stream,
But it must flow through carnage foul.
Where furies dance, and war dogs howl ?

Or, durst the muse proclaim around,
No other than " uncertain sound,"
Lest the bold strain incur the frown,
Of those who vote the faithful down ?—
Were there no men within the sphere,
By noble deed to nations dear,
Fitting to wear the laurel bays,
That poets weave when poets praise ?
No Cobden,—fearless, honest, true,
No Bright,—who boldly dare pursue
Stern duty's path, when Senates proud,
Pander to passion and the crowd ?
Were these unworthy of the strain,
That revels on the gory plain ?

Woe to the land whene'er the men,
Who strike the lyre or wield the pen,
Descend to feed and fan the flame,
That blazes with creation's shame,
Devouring with volcanic rage,
The treasures of a mighty age,
Then leaves behind a ghastly blank,
To show where wealth and virtue sank !
Woe to the men who sound the lyre,
To honour such a Nero's fire !

But deeper woe and darker gloom,
Herald a nation's coming doom,

When Heav'n-born Truth is turn'd perverse,
To justify creation's curse,
And made by Priestly art to plead
For men by whom whole nations bleed !
Go search around,—each cavern scan,
And find a blacker guilt in man.
Go dive the depths of ancient time,
Probe each recess of hidden crime,
Traverse the earth, then cross the spheres,—
Ask of the groans, the woes, the tears,
That orphans feel, that widows shed,
When battle-fields receive their dead.—
Ask Heav'n above, ask Nature round,
If guiltier deed may yet be found,
Than his, who pleads Religion's right
To hound on nations to the fight,
And who the gospel grace supplies
To him that murders while he dies ?

Thou great Eternal, God of love,
Send down thy gentle peaceful Dove.
Through the wide world henceforth inspire,
Each preacher's tongue, each poet's lyre.
Give them to plead for love to *all*,
" Who dwell on this terrestrial ball."
Give them to own a brother man,
In every tribe, in every clan.

Give them to teach with solemn awe,
Thy holy, just, and sacred law,
That man, apart from pride and pelf,
Shall love his brother as himself.
Give each to speak, give each to glow,
With sympathy for human woe ;
And where on earth that woe is known,
Give them to feel it as their own.
Give them to blot from every page,
Their plaudits of the battle's rage,
And o'er the world thy Spirit pour,
TILL POETS SING OF WAR NO MORE.

LOVE TO THE SAVIOUR.

No more, my soul, the creature love,
But fix thy thoughts on Him above,
Who suffer'd all thy pain ;
He wept and bled, and died for thee,
He bore thy sins upon the tree,
To give thee life again.

All mortal love for Him forsake,
And cheerfully his burden take,
Thy best, thy constant Friend ;

He knows thy fears, He feels thy grief,
And will apportion full relief,
　Till all thy sorrows end.

Go then, my soul, approach His Cross,
And count as lasting gain, the "loss"
　That brings thee humbly there ;
Go, seek within His open arms,
A shelter from the world's alarms,
　A refuge from despair.

See yonder happy blood-bought throng,
Hark ! how their praises pour along,
　Through all the heavenly plains ;
Archangels bear aloft the themes,
And sings the mercy that redeems,
　From everlasting pains.

Go then, my soul, go seek His love,
And let the praise of saints above,
　On earth by thee be given.
To His dear Cross with ardour cling,
And with enraptur'd sweetness sing,
　" No other way to heaven !"

LINES ON THE DEATH OF JAMES MONTGOMERY, THE
CHRISTIAN POET.

MOURN, Britain, mourn ! Thy harp unstrung,
And idly in the valley hung,
Wails to the lonely echoes there,
But wails in vain to vacant air.
The hand that raised its strains of yore,
Shall strike the silver chords no more.

In manhood's prime and early youth,
He sang of liberty and truth ;
Nor trembled at the frown of power,
Though arm'd to crush him in their hour.
He courted not to tread the halls
Of vaunting pride :—and prison walls
Carried no terror to his heart,
When duty claimed the patriot's part ;
But firm, his country's cause to plead,
He boldly came at freedom's need.

Amid the wilder notes around,
His harp gave no " uncertain sound ;"
Nor suffered he gay fashion's lure,
To tempt his muse to strains impure.
No blushless Venus soil'd his lyre,
Nor Bacchus with his sensual fire.

He sought not fame from gory plains,
Where every lawless passion reigns,
Where Death and Hell gain large renown,
By mowing mighty armies down.
His purer song raised nobler themes,
Than ever glow'd in Warrior's dreams.

Byron came on with giant stride,
Blazed with malignant heat,—and died.
Moore slaked his thirst at Eastern brook,
And drank his fill in " Lalla Rookh."
Scott, fresh from Caledonian heights,
Spent his wild power on belted knights,
Strewed o'er with dead the " Brae" and brake,
To sing his " Lady of the Lake ;"
Yet wept not, grieved not, that the flood
Ran crimson-dy'd with foemen's blood.
Coleridge and Wordsworth, noble pair !
Sang lofty themes with lofty air ;
Gave thought sublime to wondering crowds,
But soar'd too often in the clouds.
And he of " Thalaba" the bard,
Once freedom's advocate and guard,
Chose range and subject too confin'd
To converse with celestial mind.
Thus British song took wayward flight,
Too weak to reach one heavenly height ;
With wing depressed and grovelling view,
The muse despised her birth-right too.

Then rose the bard of Christian name,
To give the Muse her rightful claim,
And seize for holier theme, the bays
Too long the boast of meaner praise.
Montgomery in tender strain
Sang to the world a Saviour slain,
Confessed with mild, ingenuous pride,
To glory in the Crucified,
And show'd how all a poet's fire
Can aid " the soul's sincere desire."
The churches heard the notes divine,
And onward bore each holy line.
Across the deep the echo flew,
And distant lands the song renew ;
Till strains prepared for British child,
Are heard in Afric's desert wild ;—
And prayerful throngs admiring feel
The Poet's fire—the Christian's zeal.

Like you bold tower of princely height,
Kissed by the rays of parting light ;
Like lofty cedar seen afar,
Or as yon brilliant evening star ;
So stood the bard among his peers,
So closed his patriarchal years.

As the full shock of golden grain
Gladdens the heart of labouring swain,

Richly repays the toil and care
Through summer's heat and wintry air ;
So entered he the heavenly rest,
And took his place among the blest.

Or as some noble bark takes sail,
To brave the ocean and the gale,
Steers her bold course o'er distant seas,
Amid the tempest or the breeze ;
Then hails the port whose waters sleep,
And leaves behind the dangerous deep ;—
So reached the bard his native shore,
Where earthly billows beat no more.

Thou Poet-saint, there rest thee now,
Where care shall never cloud thy brow ;
There drink thy fill from purer stream
Than ever flow'd in human theme.
There shall thy golden harp inspire
A more than mortal poet's fire,
To strike anew the heavenly chord,
And sing "for ever with the Lord."*

---

* This quotation is from the last line reported to have been
written by the venerable poet.

THE SOLDIER.

I saw him in his childhood,
   While sporting on the green;
No sweeter bud, no lovelier flower,
   The village dames had seen.

I saw him shoot in stature,
   The tallest of his race ;
He carried greatness in his mien,
   And beauty in his face.

I saw him in his manhood,
   A noble man was he ;
He stood confess'd, the bravest there—
   The freest of the free.

I saw him when deluded,
   By words of dark deceit ;
He little thought that words so fair
   Were spoken by a cheat.

I saw him clothed in scarlet,
   With gaudy plume and lace ;
He sat upon a noble steed,
   With yet more noble grace.

I saw him after battle,
  To misery doomed for life ;
He rued the day when first he heard
  The sound of drum and fife.

I saw him wan and wretched,
  A cripple, begging bread ;
The "pamper'd menial" drove him forth.
  With curses on his head.

I saw his last lone dwelling,
  The rags and broken stool ;
He breath'd out dying words and said,
  ' The soldier is a fool !"

NOTES.

" Never shall I forget my unceremonious installation into this novel piece of furniture; this curiously wrought, though ill-shaped, piece of timber—this 'National Testimonial'—this trophy of War, which I had won by deeds of arms. [A wooden leg.] When fitted on, strapped by the knee, and girt at the waist to painful annoyance, I looked down in sullen silence at the hated appendage, with about the same kind of satisfaction as a dog does when he gets a tin kettle tied to his tail."—*Life of Thomas Jackson, late Sergeant of the Coldstream Guards. p.* 119.

" One day that I was going about the town (Walsall) for that purpose, [*i. e.* for employment] I met with the first cutting insult on my misfortune, such as I had anticipated to be realised by

E 2

the vulgar in my own town. In passing a group of the unwashed, assembled at an idle corner, as they all gaped on me, one said, -'Ho's he?' Another answered, 'Why, don't you know him? —he's young Jackson, as went into the Militia, and then he must volunteer to go and see war, and they'n sarved him out for it.' 'Sarves him right,' says another, 'he had no business there.'"—*Ibid. p.* 123.

"And this is the end!" he muttered, in broken accents—"the end of a soldier's life!—left here to die, like a worn-out and useless hound! Better have been killed outright than left thus!" ...."Fool that I was!" continued he, not heeding her words, (his wife)—I *would* be a soldier, a man!—and now I am worse than a sickly woman,—wounded, lame, dying!—and deserted by those who brought me to this."—*The Soldier's Progress, p.* 102.

TO THE GENIUS OF WAR.

AS EMBODIED IN THE WARRIOR.

FORBEAR, thou man of blood, forbear,
    To claim a birth Divine ;
No Son of Heaven can be the heir
    Of passions such as thine.

Thy boasted trade, thy sole employ,
    Is death to deal around ;
The Peace of nations to destroy,
    Wherever man is found.

The wide-spread earth, through all her lands,
   Has mourned thy kindred tread ;
And widows raise their pray'rful hands,
   For vengeance on thy head.

In Europe's polished courts, the seeds
   Of hatred thou hast sown ;
And yonder Southern island bleeds*
   With sorrows all thine own.

In thronging East, or far-spread West,
   Or where the Niger rolls ;
Thy murd'rous train has proved the pest
   And curse, of human souls.

No sex, no nation, and no clime,
   Has 'scap'd thy cruel rage ;
Thy plague has flow'd throughout all time,
   And spread through every age.

And shall that plague, with curses rife,
   Pass down to other times ;
And spread around the seeds of strife,
   To poison other climes?

---

* Otaheite.

Shall men be found for wealth or gain,
   To doom a world to woe?
And all that earth can feel of pain,
   Give earth that all to know?

Learn, then, O man to murder given,
   Note thou the mandate well;
"The work of Peace came down from heaven,
   The work of War from hell."

SUNDAY, AND SUNDAY BANDS.

No. 1.

"Remember the Sabbath day, to keep it holy."

Thou day of God, best gift of Heaven,
   The gem and glory of the seven;
Thou type of purer world and blest,
Where Saints in holy service rest;
Thee will I hail—thee dearly prize,
Thou sweetest emblem of the skies.

   For me, no "Sunday Bands" shall play,
To "wile" thy precious hours away;
In vain for me the "Park" shall spread,
Its beauties to allure my tread;

In vain the gay " Saloon" and crowd,
With boisterous mirth and laughter loud ;
In vain they tempt with pomp and glare,
My soul can seek no portion there.
Their flowing sounds, their giddy mirth,
No higher rise than sinful earth.

O day of God,—thy lovely hours,
Shall be to me as Eden's bowers ;
Whose calm retreats and holy rest,
Make earth itself, like Heaven, blest.
Here I enjoy a sweet repose,
Beyond the reach of secret foes.
Here I converse with Him who died,
And glory in the crucified.
Here, Enoch-like, I walk with God,
And trace the path the prophets trod.
Here I descry though far away,
The glories of a heavenly day;
Here too I leave all earthly care,
To find a sweet relief in prayer,
And sing, that in a world bereft,
We have so much of Heaven left.

And shall I seize for sinful mirth,
The hours the Saviour claims on earth ?
And give to "Sunday Bands" and pride,
The sacred time of Him who died ?

Or yield the day that saw Him rise.
To aught of joy below the skies ?

No ! Never be this holy day,
The sport for " Sunday Bands" to play.
Never be sacred hours like these,
Bestowed on Parks and spreading trees.
And Never, Never, be the boon,
Devoted to the vile Saloon.
Rather than this, may Britain be
Blotted from living memory;
Rather than this, may ruin rend
This solid globe from end to end ;
Rather than this, ye rolling spheres,
For ever close our mortal years,
And loud proclaim with Him of yore,
That guilty " Time shall be no more."

SUNDAY, AND SUNDAY BANDS.

No. 2.

(*Written in reply to an Infidel attack on the foregoing Piece.*)

" —— and call the Sabbath a delight, the holy of the Lord,
honourable; and shalt honour him, not doing thine own
ways, NOR FINDING THINE OWN PLEASURE, nor speaking
thine own words."—Isa. lviii. 13.

LET bold impiety deride,
With boasting insolence and pride ;

And bandy forth the vulgar charge,
That hireling Sceptics deal at large ;
No scorn of their's can blot the claim.
Of Him by whom Creation came ;
Nor jeers nor banter wrest Ilis day,
For Godless " Sunday Bands" to play.

Know, impious man, that He alone,
Who reigns on Heaven's Eternal Throne ;
Has power and right a day to claim,
In honour of His Holy name.
That day He claimed when time was young,
When sinless earth His glory sung ;
That day He claimed with solemn awe,
When Sinai's thunders gave the law ;
That day, now doubly dear on earth,
The seal of nature's second birth,
When Love, that stoop'd to die, arose,
And prostrate laid his vanquish'd foes,
—He claims anew, for holy rest,
As type and foretaste of the blest.

And now vain man, select the age,
From Sacred or Historic page,
And show what nation knew decay,
That bravely kept this Holy day ?
See Judah rise to pomp and power,
Of nations then the pride and flower ;

Her Kings, by wisdom and renown,
Shed lustre on her noble crown.
See vengeance drive her forth, and doom
Her cities to unbroken gloom,
And "seventy years" of captive toil
Pass o'er her head on foreign soil ;
Then ask her crime?   Ask why that yoke?
But Centuries of Sabbaths broke?

And where around rests Heaven's smile?
Is it where "Sunday Bands" beguile?
In solemn Spain, Italia gay,
Or where Vienna's triflers play?
Is it where frolic and the dance,
Unite to bless a Holy France?
Where "silken hues, the smell of flowers,
The loveliness of sylvan bowers,"
With nymphs and beauty ever dwell,
Yet " want but flame to make it hell ?"*

---

* A few years ago the writer spent a Sunday in the City of
Paris.   Aware of the scenes presented on that holy day in the
French capital, he did not leave his Hotel but for Divine worship.
Early in the evening, an English fellow-traveller came in and
enquired, " Have you been in the *Champs D'Elysees* this evening?"
To which the writer replied, "No."   Then he remarked, "Oh,
you should go and see it, for *it wants nothing but the flame to
make it hell !*"—He afterwards stated that there were Bands,

Where jovial crowds in pleasure drown,
The shame of freedom trampled down ?
Thou land of fiddling, gay Voltaire,
Say, can we find Heaven's blessing there ?
No,—Heaven's blessing takes its flight,
Where States deny the Sabbath right ;
And History proclaims abroad,
Who keep no Sabbath—have no God !

O Thou my lov'd, my native land,
Britain, by whom nor Sunday Band,
Nor Sunday theatre allowed,
Has soil'd thy bright escutcheon proud :
Sooner than thou should'st lose thy power,
I'd fain invoke thy fatal hour ;
Sooner than thou should'st sin like France
With Sunday bands and Sunday dance,
May earth be wrapp'd in endless gloom,
And nature meet her final doom.
O heed not those who sing of trees,
Of dulcet sounds, with flowing breeze ;
Who praise the fields, and fruits, and flowers,
The spreading lawn, and sylvan bowers ;

Theatres, Saloons, Mountebanks, Jugglers, Dancers, &c. &c. all
surrounded with crowds who appeared to be highly gratified.
Such is the kind of Sabbath to which the spirit of Sunday Bands
would eventually conduct this Christian land ! !

Who tell you there to pass away,
The hours of Heaven's own Holy day,
Who " Nature" make their Great High Priest :—
Thus sang Tom Paine,—then died a beast !

STANZAS ADDRESSED TO MELROSE ABBEY.

THOU mighty shade of unknown age !
 Thou tomb of monarch, saint, and sage !
Whose vacant aisles, and tottering wall,
On dark sepulchral echoes call ;
Beneath whose gloomy crumbling tower,
The nightshade and the nettle, flower ;
And gobblins dance, or spectres play,
Where hooded monks once knelt to pray.

Though great in ruins, great in fame,
No marble marks thy builder's name ;
And vainly, through thy space, I seek
His shrine who made thy pillars speak ;
And chisselled into life the stone
That leaves the workman all unknown ;
His more than Phidian skill I trace,
But seek in vain that Phidian's place.*

---

* By those who have visited and *examined* this splendid ruin,
the following description of the matchless excellence of its

Say, noble ruin ! fane sublime!
Who floating down the stream of time,
When kilted tribe and mountain clan
Sow'd deadly hate 'twixt man and man,
And shouted "Glory !" to the Gael,
Who pour'd fell murder through the vale :—
Say, who among the mighty dead,
For *virtue* or for *freedom* bled ?

Alone and silent, here, I stray,
While moon-beams with thy arches play ;
And memory the age recalls,
When battle raged about thy walls ;
When "border" hate, and "tartan" strife,
Quaff'd deep the blood of foeman's life ;
When " pibroch" rang the hills around,
As death stalked ghastly o'er the ground :—

But who for virtuous *freedom* died ?
Who, trampling on the warrior's pride,

workmanship, by no mean authority, will not be considered
an exaggeration.

" In some of the cloisters there are representations of flowers,
vegetables, &c., carved in stone with accuracy and precision so
delicate, that we almost distrust our senses, when we consider
the difficulty of subjecting so hard a substance to such intricate
and exquisite modulation."—*Lay of the Last Minstrel, Note* 2:,
Canto 1.

Bore witness, as he drew the steel,
His quarrel was the " public weal ?"
That he but sought the dreadful hour,
Alone to crush the despot's power,
And his brave arm should strike no blow,
But laid some " proud oppressor low ?"

Alas ! the warrior's boasted rage,
In ancient or in modern age,
In savage tribe, or well-trained band,
Is not to guard the freeman's land.
For trivial cause, for paltry hire,
He sets his angry soul on fire,
And maniac-like, with Deloraine,
For wizard's falsehood scours the plain.

Fair Melrose ! ere thy mouldering wall
Shall tremble to its final fall ;
Ere ruin, in her dreaded hour,
Shall prostrate smite thy solemn tower ;
Or " Walter," with his " Michael" Scott,
In dark oblivion are forgot,
This song shall roll creation o'er,
" The nations now learn war no more."

LINES ADDRESSED TO A SLANDERER.

" But the tongue can no man tame ; it is an unruly evil, full
of deadly poison."—James iii. 8.

FLY, caitiff, fly the haunts of men,
And hide thee in thy native den ;
Go, seek thy home in deserts foul,
Where serpents hiss and tigers howl.

Meet messmates these for such as thee,
And meet the scenes that yield them glee !
Go, join them in their cruel feasts,
And be the well-met friend of beasts.

There shalt thou find congenial deeds,
For there the helpless victim bleeds ;
There shalt thou learn to deal the blow
That lays his hated virtue low. ·

The serpent there, in secret lurk,
Shall teach thee well to do thy work—
The dark retreat, the hidden guile,
And how to poison with a smile.

He'll teach thee when the oily tongue
Shall be with friendly phrases strung ;
He'll teach thee, too, with wondrous skill,
How best to flatter while you kill.

The tiger, too, shall thee befriend,
And teach thee how the weak to rend ;
How to secrete the foul intent,
When on the work of ruin bent.

Thus taught, go blast thy victim's fame,
Behind his back pollute his name ;
In whisper'd softness spread disgrace
But *never meet him face to face.*

Let him not see the hand that smites,
Let him not feel the tooth that bites ;
Let him not know that friendship's breath,
Conveys the poisoned air of death.

Thus do thy work thou monster foul,
Where serpents hiss, and tigers howl ;
But keep thee to thy native den,
Nor curse again the haunts of men.*

---

* The Gospel rule, if generally practised, would speedily destroy this unworthy and pernicious spirit of defamation. It may be safely affirmed that this *secret slander*, this cowardly weapon of weak or wicked men, has done more injury to domestic society, and broken more hearts, than any other social vice. It infects all circles, corrupts all companies, and pollutes all associations. Even Christian ministers are too prone to indulge in it, not so much by *direct* defamation, as by inuendo, *whisperings*, insinuations disguised in a candid verbiage, and

LINES ADDRESSED TO THE ISLE OF MAN.

Thou gem of the Ocean, thou pearl of the Sea,
  Whose rock-begirt shores are the Home of the Free;
Thou Queen among Islands, though small thy domain,
I love thy fair sceptre, and leave thee with pain.

Full oft have I roamed o'er thy native delights,
Thy soft flowing dells, or thy cloud-crested heights;
Or sooth'd by the "Douglas," have follow'd the stream,
Where lovers may whisper, or poets may dream.

And each rolling season that gives me once more
To view thy bold outline and tread thy sweet shore;

"Have you heard?" "Is it true?" &c., where in the shape of enquiry the scandal is intentionally spread by the very question put. Why not be honest and *go direct to the suspected party?* Why not act a manly part and acquaint him with the injurious report, and ask for an explanation? Why stab the man *behind his back,* or ruin him *in the dark?* It is base, cowardly, and unchristian. Let ministers and *all* Christians *insist* on the following beautiful rule; "Moreover, if thy brother shall trespass against thee, go and tell him his fault *between thee and him alone;* if he shall hear thee, thou hast gained thy brother," Matt. xviii. 15. This conduct invariably pursued, would speedily render wholly unnecessary the severity of the above censure, by removing the cause which gave it birth; but so long as the poison is spread by designing, or thoughtless, or wicked men, no condemnation of it can be too severe.

F

Endears thee anew, like some friend, to my heart,
From whom it may never, no, never depart.

For what though the haughty and proud may disdain,
To bow to thy sceptre and hallow thy reign ;
What though giddy fashion may seek other skies,
Thou hast, O fair Mona ! a lovelier prize.

Oh Labour ! thou Nurse of our national Health,
Thou spring-head of Commerce, and parent of Wealth ;
Thou glory of Britain,—thy children, when free,
Are lovely as princes to Mona and me.

Whene'er in the day of their freedom they roam,
Their smiles spread around them the Englishman's home ;
And no gilded coronet graces the soil,
Like the bold manly forms of these children of toil.

Upon thy fair bosom, thou gem of the West !
Long, long may these thousands be welcome, and blest ;
And be it thy glory, wherever they roam,
That Mona can find them an Englishman's Home.

LITTLE JENNY, OR THE CONTENTED COTTAGER.

I SAT on the stile by the rich waving corn,
  And drank the sweet air in the pride of the morn ;
The lark broke from slumbers and soar'd beyond sight,
But pour'd ceaseless music from regions of light.

A prim little maiden came tripping along,
And sweet was her blue eye, but sweeter her song ;
She glanced at the stranger,—her look seemed to say,
'Sir, let me pass over nor hinder my way.'

That look was a study, and spoke of her haste,
Unconscious that maiden of guile or of " taste,"
Her ringlets of auburn flowed wild on the air,
And innocence reigned on that countenance fair.

I said, " Little maiden, you're happy to day,
You sing as yon lark which is soaring away ;"
" O yes Sir," she answered, " I cannot be sad,
With so much around me to make my heart glad.

" Yon cottage you see by the side of the hill.
With the woodbine around it and close by the rill,
That, Sir, is my home—and no home is so fair,
For father, and mother, and baby are there."

" But maiden your cottage looks humble and low,
'Tis not like the mansion you passed on that brow :
That mansion is large, and its rooms are so fine,
A palace, compared to that cottage of thine."

" O Sir," said the maiden, " no stranger can tell,
What sweetness resides in the home where I dwell ;
That mansion is larger and finer to see,
Yet never can equal that cottage to me.

" My father he loves me, and I love him too,
He often says, " Jenny, a warm kiss for you ;"
And mother, she speaks in a language so mild,
And calls me her Jenny, her own little child.

" And baby,—his name, Sir, is Johnny, you know,—
He also is happy and smiles at me too ;
And when mother tells me to give him his food,
He looks like an angel, so sweet, and so good.

" O Sir, I do think you are wrong when you say,
My cottage is not like that mansion so gay ;
No mansion is like it, no palace so fair,
When father, and mother, and baby are there."

I saw I had touch'd a sad chord in her heart,
And said, " Little maiden, before you depart,
I tell you you're right, and wherever you roam,
No place will you love like that sweet cottage home.

" Yon mansion looks down on that humble hill side,
And wears a bold front as it frowns in its pride ;
But, maiden, the humble, content with their lot,
Find heaven on earth in the lowliest cot."

" O yes, Sir," she said, as she curtsied away,
" My father and mother have taught me to pray ;
And often they tell me that life when well spent,
Will make any cottage the home of content."

LINES ON THE DEATH OF MR. OWEN JOHNSON,

Who departed this life on Tuesday evening, August 16, 1853, in the ninetieth year of his age, having been a member of the Baptist Church, Cannon Street, Birmingham, during the long period of seventy-two years, for nearly thirty-nine of which he honourably sustained the office of Deacon.

HAIL, friendly Death ! No King of terrors thou !
No frowning vengeance settles on thy brow.
No gloomy horrors follow in thy train,
Since Christ has triumphed and " to die is gain."
Nor will we weep, or shed one useless tear,
While gather'd round the sainted father's bier.

True he has gone, and yonder house of prayer*
No more shall witness his devotions there ;
His favourite seat, for threescore years and ten,
Shall never be his favourite seat again ;
That long-accustomed, honoured spot shall be,
The cenotaph to Johnson's memory.
Nor more his aged patriarchal form,
Like noble oak that bends before the storm,
Shall lead the way beneath the weight of years,
To His loved throne who wipes the mourner's tears :
No more shall he, with mild, delighted eye,
Pour the warm prayer to Him who rules the sky,

* Cannon Street Chapel.

Or at the festal board of Him who died,
'Mid thronging brethren, sing " Christ crucified."
No more, with heaven beaming in his face,
The Patriarch Saint shall take official place.

But shall we mourn that he at length ascends,
To holier service and to lovelier friends ?
That now, escap'd from suffering and complaint,
The earthly, rises to the heavenly, Saint?
That he, who long on Canaan's border stood,
Has cross'd the Jordan and outlived the flood ?
No.   Tears and sorrow from the scene retire,
When patriarch fathers mount their car of fire.

Let faith pursue the heaven-directed flight,
And see him enter on the realms of light.
Who first advancing from that white-rob'd throng,
Whose holy raptures pour th' extatic song,
To golden melody on earth unknown,
And sung to none but Him upon the throne ?
What angel-spirit, with cherubic love,
Welcomes the pilgrim to the plains above,
And stepping forth that well-known form to greet,
Conducts him onward to the Saviour's feet,
Where bending low with sacred joy and fear,
Exclaims, " Behold, my friend and father here ?"
'Tis holy Pearce!—his seraph, loving eye
Has often scann'd the arrivals at the sky,
And look'd and long'd for yet another there,
With whom full oft he join'd in mighty prayer.

And now they meet,—but who their bliss supernal,
Their gushing joy—ineffable—eternal,
In thought can ponder, or in words convey,
Amidst the shadows of our mortal day ?
Forbear, my Muse, the vain attempt forbear,
Lest utter darkness shroud thee in despair.

With golden harp and sweet celestial song,
There gather round a bright familiar throng ;
A princely band, who, fir'd with heavenly love,
Greet his glad entrance to the realms above,
And eager tell it to the hosts around,
That unto death he faithful still was found.
There noble Fuller, Ryland, Ward, and King,
Hail him their friend, and notes of victory sing ;
There Carey, Thomas, Sutcliff, Birt, and Hall,
Adore anew the Sov'reign Lord of All,
While herald tongues proclaim through all the host,
" Another saint has reached the heavenly coast."

Adieu, thou veteran saint, awhile adieu,
God is thy glory and thy portion too.
Safe in His kingdom and amid thy peers,
We mourn thee not, nor shed unholy tears.
Thy work is done, thy night of conflict past,
Thy struggle o'er, the longest and the last.
We watched thy ascent, saw the opening day,
And heard the whisper, " Spirit come away !"
By faith we saw the "ministering" band,
Arrive to bear thee to their native land.

But as they wing'd thee far from earthly woe,
Say, fell thy mantle on a saint below ?
Or, as thy glory parts thee from our view,
Say, have we lost thy sacred mantle too ?
   Now to the grave thy "MORTAL" we convey,
Dark is the passage that leads on to day ;
Yet breaks that day full joyous through the gloom,
And shews death vanquished in the silent tomb ;
With shattered sceptre, and with broken pride,
Crush'd at his feet who conquered when He died.
Exclaim we now, " O Death, where is thy sting ?"
And on the borders of his empire sing :

    " Here we leave in lonely keeping
      Of the dark and silent grave ;
   All that saints can know of sleeping,
      'Till He comes who comes to save.

    " And His eye, still watching o'er thee,
      Counts each particle of dust ;
   He, in passing through before thee,
      Made thy grave a sacred trust.

    " Joyous, then, we leave thee sleeping ;
      Safely rest till He shall call,
   Then come forth from earthly keeping,
      Come, and crown Him Lord of All.

"Lord of All, we now adore Thee,
   Guardian of our mould'ring clay ;
Living, be our only glory,
   Dying, be our endless stay."

LINES

*Written on the Funeral of J. Wright, Esq., late of Sparkbrook,
Birmingham, who died May 2nd, 1854, aged fifty-five years.
He was a man of eminent benevolence, and of large-hearted
charity towards all sects and parties of Christians. His
funeral was attended by mourning crowds of the working
classes and others, by whom he was held in high esteem.*

THE bell sounds mournful through the gloom,
   That hovers o'er the open tomb ;
While care and sorrow mark the mein,
Of throngs who gather round the scene,
Where " men devout" their friend convey,
To mingle with the silent clay.

The aged there bent low with years,
And widows, mingle honest tears ;
Childhood and youth alike deplore,
" That they shall see his face no more."
While unwashed crowds their toils suspend,
And weep that they have lost a friend.

More noble this than boasted name,
Deep buried in Heraldic fame ;
With "Centaur," "Gamb," and "Sphynx" entwirled,
Like relics of a former world ;
Or " Star," and " Gyphon," " Vest," and " Gu,"
As ancient, and as useless too.

No Herald pomp, no marble bust,
Records the deeds of mouldering dust,
Like living hearts, whose treasured thought,
Of hunger fed and childhood taught,
Shall nurse the fond undying fame,
With lasting blessings on his name.

And such was Wright, to sect or creed
His manly heart showed little heed ;
His own he prized with tender care,
And fixed a warm affection there ;
But far beyond,—his purse, his all,
He freely gave at duty's call.

Peace to thee, saint ! thy work is done,
And heaven has called its faithful son ;
Of bless'd rewards take there thy fill,
We claim thy bright example still ;
And this shall be thy motto'd crest,
" The memory of the just is bless'd."

LINES ON THE DEATH OF JOSEPH STURGE, ESQ.

(Late of Birmingham,)

Who departed this life on Saturday, May 16, 1859, in the
sixty-sixth year of his age.

" Know ye not that there is a prince and a great man fallen this
day in Israel ?"—2 Sam. iii. 38.

CLOUDS dense and dark hang o'er the land,
  And ocean surges on the strand ;
The hurrying crowd in whispers low,
Spread silently the nation's woe.
Fathers with sadness tell the grief,
And mothers seek, in tears, relief ;
Grave senators forego debate,
To join the mourning of the State.

Why sorrow thus,—so wide, so deep ?
Why should a mighty nation weep ?
Why through the church, the crowd, the press,
Should Britain bow in keen distress ?
Why the complaint in hall and cot,
Of loss that cannot be forgot ?
And why from noble to the swain,
Is heard the moan,—and felt the pain ?

" Know ye not," then, that he who gave,
His heart and purse, to free the slave ;—

That he who toil'd to snap his chain,
And raise him to a man again ;
That he who spent a life to be,
The living friend of liberty ;
Is now no more ?—His princely day,
Has done its work, and pass'd away.

He, great in deeds,—not words or speech,
But great in deeds, that live to teach,
Has closed his day, but leaves behind,
A noble pattern for mankind.
No narrow end, no selfish aim,
Tarnished the honour of his name.
Nor knew he life but as a plan,
To work the highest good of man.

Now view that pattern,—see it stand,
Like solid rock amid the land ;
Or as some pyramidal form,
Braving the tempest and the storm ;
Imperial goodness at the base,
With wide-spread love for human race,
While virtues upon virtues rise,
To bear the apex to the skies.

On sable Afric's distant coast,
That name remains a pride and boast ;

And through yon beauteous Western Isle,*
It passes for a household smile.
Mothers and children sing with glee,
Of him who work'd to set them free,
And now united sorrows pour,
That they shall see his face no more.

Turn to the North,—his mem'ry there,
Is sweet as balm upon the air.
The Dane and Russ revere the name,
Of him who sought to quench the flame
Of cruel war, and stay the deed,
That made ten thousand widows bleed.
They spurn the men who laugh'd to scorn,
That lovely act as frenzied born.

Adieu, thou friend of human right,
Thy Country mourns thy sudden flight,
Nor knows who yet with equal grace,
Shall rise to fill thy noble place.
Thy life of love,—thy deeds sublime,
Shall treasured be by rolling time ;
And ages, to its farthest verge,
Shall bless the name of Joseph Sturge.

* Jama'ca.

BRIEF MEMOIR OF THE PUBLIC LIFE OF MR. JOSEPH STURGE.

JOSEPH STURGE was born at Elberton, in the county of Gloucester, on the 2nd of August, 1793. He was the second son of Joseph Sturge, a farmer of that place, and was the sixth in direct succession who bore that name. On coming of age, he established himself in business at Bewdley, as a corn merchant, and removed to Birmingham about the year 1822. We need scarcely say that by dint of enterprise, energy, and integrity, he and his brother succeeded in establishing one of the first houses in England; the business done by their firm constituting a large proportion of the trade of the port of Gloucester, where their warehouses are chiefly situated.

In 1837, Mr. Sturge undertook a voyage to Jamaica, in order to examine with his own eyes the actual condition of the Negroes, and to ascertain the true character of the Apprenticeship Clause in the Emancipation Act. To his honest and fearless exposure of the cruelties and oppressions perpetrated under that deceptive clause, it was very greatly, if not mainly owing, that the apprenticeship system was brought to a close, and complete Emancipation accomplished much earlier than would otherwise have been the case. His appalling details opened the eyes of the whole nation, and aroused a feeling of indignation before which the last remains of West Indian Slavery were ultimately compelled to retreat. The eminent service he thus rendered to the Negro race entitles his memory to take rank with Wilberforce, Clarkson, Buxton, and other distinguished friends of humanity and freedom. He was a large contributor to the Jamaica Baptist Education Society, and there was scarcely an effort made to benefit the African race to which he did not yield his great influence and liberal support.

Such missions of good-will as these brought Mr. Sturge before the public of late years, but in his own town and neighbourhood he was always at work. No Birmingham man will have for-gotten his earnest efforts to mitigate the effects, and to unravel the causes of the riots of 1840, and to restore to the Corporation that constitutional control over the police of which they were unjustly deprived under the influence of the groundless terrors which those riots occasioned. He established and maintained at his own expense the first reformatory set on foot in the Midland district; he took great personal interest in the Severn-street Schools; doing duty as a superintendent Sunday after Sunday. He devoted several acres of valuable land to the purpose of a free play-ground for the working classes; he was president of the Birmingham Temperance Society, president of the Band of Hope Union, and always ready to give counsel and substantial aid to every practical scheme of social improvement. A few days before his death he sent the Birmingham and Midland Institute a cheque for £100. The extent of his private charities and good deeds was only known to himself.

In 1850, Mr. Sturge, accompanied by Mr. Elihu Burritt, and Mr. Frederick Wheeler, proceeded to Schleswig-Holstein, with a view of inducing the authorities there to terminate the war with Denmark by referring the whole dispute to the arbitration of some enlightened and impartial persons who might be mutually agreed upon. This mission of love arose out of an eloquent appeal by Dr. Bodenstadt, of Berlin, addressed to the Peace Congress at Frankfort-on-the-Maine, entreating that body to appoint a commission of inquiry into the points at issue between Denmark and the Duchies. As it was beyond the province of that Congress to assume the exercise of governmental functions, they respectfully declined the application, upon which Mr. Sturge and his two friends *in their private capacity* undertook to intercede with the belligerents on behalf of the pacific interests of their repective people. It was truly a "work of faith and a labour of love," undertaken in the spirit of Christianity, and prosecuted with an earnestness, zeal, and wisdom, which, to say the least, deserved a complete success.

THE VISIT OF MR. STURGE, TO ST. PETERSBURG RESPECTING THE RUSSIAN WAR, 1854.

Mr. Sturge, having been appointed by the Society of Friends (*not* by the Peace Society as numbers have erroneously supposed and asserted) in conjunction with Mr. Henry Pease, of Darlington, and Mr. Robert Charleton, of Bristol, a deputation to present an address to the Emperor, which had been adopted by that Society, set out on this benevolent mission on the 20th of January, 1854, in the coldest part of the year. They travelled through Berlin, Königsberg, and Riga, to St. Petersburg. On the 10th of February, they were admitted to an audience with the Emperor, by whom they were received with great kindness, who listened to their memorial with close attention, and who made a suitable reply, which is given below. The deputation reached London on their return on Thursday evening, February 23rd with the conscious satisfaction of having attempted, amid many difficulties and much contumely, to avert a great calamity from mankind.

ADDRESS FROM THE RELIGIOUS SOCIETY OF FRIENDS TO THE EMPEROR OF RUSSIA.

To NICHOLAS, *Emperor of all the Russias.*

" May it please the Emperor,

" We, the undersigned, Members of a Meeting representing the religious Society of Friends (commonly called Quakers,) in Great Britain, venture to approach the Imperial presence, under a deep conviction of religious duty, and in the constraining love of Christ our Saviour.

"We are moreover encouraged so to do, by the many proofs of condescension and Christian kindness manifested by thy late illustrious brother, the Emperor Alexander, as well as by thy honoured mother, to some of our brethren in religious profession.

"It is well known that, apart from all political considerations, we have, as a Christian church, uniformly upheld a testimony against war, on the simple ground that it is utterly condemned by the precepts of Christianity, as well as altogether incompatible with the spirit of its Divine Founder, who is emphatically styled the 'Prince of Peace.' This conviction we have repeatedly pressed upon our own rulers, and often, in the language of bold but respectful remonstrance, have we urged upon them the maintenance of Peace, as the true policy, as well as manifest duty, of a Christian government.

"And now, O Great Prince, permit us to express the sorrow which fills our hearts, as Christians and as men, in contemplating the probability of war in any portion of the continent of Europe. Deeply to be deplored would it be were that peace which to a very large extent has happily prevailed so many years, exchanged for the unspeakable horrors of war, with all its attendant moral evil and physical suffering.

"It is not our business, nor do we presume to offer any opinion upon the questions now at issue between the Imperial Government of Russia and that of any other country; but estimating the exalted position in which Divine Providence has placed thee, and the solemn responsibilities devolving upon thee, not only as an earthly potentate, but also as a believer in that Gospel which proclaims 'peace on earth,' and 'goodwill toward

G

men,' we implore Him, by whom Kings reign and Princes decree justice,' so to influence thy heart and to direct thy councils at this momentous crisis, that thou mayest practically exhibit to the nations, and even to those who do not profess the 'like precious faith,' the efficacy of the Gospel of Christ, and the universal application of his command, 'Love your enemies; bless them that curse you ; do good to them that hate you ; and pray for them which despitefully use you and persecute you; that ye may be the children of your Father which is in Heaven.'

"The more fully the Christian is persuaded of the justice of his own cause, the greater his magnanimity in the exercise of forbearance. May the Lord make thee the honoured instrument of exemplifying this true nobility; thereby securing to thyself and to thy vast dominions that true glory and those rich blessings which could never result from the most successful appeal to arms.

"Thus, O mighty Prince, may the miseries and devastation of war be averted ; and, in that solemn day when "every one of us shall give account of himself to God,' may the benediction of the Redeemer apply to thee, 'Blessed are the peacemakers, for they shall be called the children of God,' and mayest thou be permitted through a Saviour's love to exchange an earthly for a heavenly crown—'a crown of glory which fadeth not away.'"

London, First Month 11, 1854.

_____

While the Deputation read this Address, the Emperor listened with marked attention. He then expressed a wish to offer some explanation of the circumstances which had led to the present unhappy dispute, and spoke nearly as follows :—

"We received the blessings of Christianity from the Greek Empire, and this has established, and maintained ever since, a link of connection, both moral and religious, between Russia and that Power. The ties that have thus united the two countries have subsisted for 900 years, and were not severed by the conquest of Russia by the Tartars ;—and when at a later period, our country succeeded in shaking off that yoke, and the Greek Empire, in its turn, fell under the sway of the Turks, we still continued to take a lively interest in the welfare of our co-religionists there : and when Russia became powerful enough to resist the Turks, and to dictate the terms of peace, we paid particular attention to the well-being of the Greek Church, and procured the insertion in successive treaties, of most important articles in her favour. I have, myself, acted as my predecessors had done, and the Treaty of Adrianople, in 1829, was as explicit as the former ones in this respect. Turkey, on her part, recog. nized this right of religious interference, and fulfilled her engagements until within the last year or two, when, for the first time she gave me reason to complain. I will not advert to the parties who were her principal instigators on that occasion ; suffice it to say, that it became my duty to interfere, and to claim from Turkey the fulfilment of her engagements. My representations were pressing but friendly, and I have every reason to believe that matters would soon have been settled, if Turkey had not been induced by other parties to believe that I had ulterior objects in view; that I was aiming at conquest, aggrandizement, and the ruin of Turkey. I have solemnly disclaimed, and do so now as solemnly disclaim, every such motive. I do not desire war ; I abhor it as sincerely as you do, and am ready to forget the past, if only the opportunity be afforded me.

I have great esteem for your country, and a sincere affection for your Queen, whom I admire not only as a Sovereign, but as a lady, a wife, and a mother. 1 have placed full confidence in her, and have acted towards her in a frank and friendly spirit. I felt it my duty to call her attention to future dangers, which I

considered as likely sooner or later to arise in the East, in consequence of the existing state of things. What on my part was
prudent foresight, has been unfairly construed in your country
into a designing policy, and an ambitious desire of conquest.
This has deeply wounded my feelings and afflicted my heart.
Personal insults and invectives I regard with indifference. It is
beneath my dignity to notice them. And I am ready to forgive
all that is personal to me, and to hold out my hand to my
enemies in the true Christian spirit. I cannot understand what
cause of complaint your nation has against Russia. I am
anxious to avoid war by all possible means—I will not attack,
and shall only act in self-defence ; but I cannot be indifferent
to what concerns the honour of my country. I have a duty to
perform as a Sovereign. As a Christian, I am ready to comply
with the precepts of religion. On the present occasion, my great
duty is to attend to the interests and honour of my country."

The deputation received also from Count Nesselrode the
following official answer :—

Sa Majesté l'Empereur a reçu l'Adresse présentée par la
Députation de la Société des Amis avec une vive satisfaction,
comme l'expression de sentiments entièrement conformes à ceux
dont il est animé lui-même. Sa Majesté a horreur comme eux
de la guerre et désire sincèrement le maintien de la paix.
Pour y arriver elle est prête à oublier les insultes et les
offenses personelles, à tendre le premier la main à ses ennemis
et à faire toutes les concessions compatibles avec l'honneur.
Sa Majesté n'attaquera pas : elle ne fera que se défendre, et sera
toujours disposée à entendre des offres de paix.

L'Empereur regrette vivement l'état actuel des choses, et il
en rejette loin de lui la responsabilité. Il a constamment
désiré vivre en bonne entente avec l'Angleterre : il a une
sincère affection pour la Reine, qu'il estime comme Souveraine,

Femme, Epouse, et Mère ; et Il lui a donné des preuves non équivoques de confiance et d'égards. Sa Majesté répudie toute idée ambitieuse de conquête ou d'ingérence injuste dans les affaires de la Turquie : elle n'y réclame que ce qu'elle a le droit de démander en vertu des traités explicites conclus par ses dévanciers et par elle-même. Le lieu qui unit la Russie à ses co-religionnaires en Orient dâte d'il y a 900 ans ; c'est de l'ancien Empire Grec que lui est venue le Christianisme, et depuis ce tems une communauté constante d'intérèts religieux à été maintenue entre la Russie et l'Empire de Byzance jusqu'à sa chûte. Débarrassée elle-même du joug des Tartares, la Russie s'est depuis ce tems constamment appliquée à améliorer le sort de ses co-religionnaires : Elle y a travaillé avec succès. Elle ne saurait récuser ses sympathies religieuses pour eux et renoncer à une influence légitime acquise au prix de son sang. Mais l'Empereur ne veut rien au delà : Il n'en veut nullement aux Turcs : et il serait heureux de voir l'Angleterre rendre meilleure justice au mobile qui a guidé ses actions. Il ne croit pas lui avoir jamais donné le moindre motif de plainte, et il en appelle au témoignage de tous les Anglais établis dans ce pays, qui n'hésiterout pas (Sa Majesté en est convaincue,) à déclarer qu'ils n'ont eu toujours qu' à se louer de l'accueil qu'ils ont trouvé en Russie.   (Signed)   NESSELRODE.

Petersbourg, le $\frac{1}{13}$ Fevrier, 1854.

AFFECTIONATE REMEMBRANCE OF MR. STURGE IN JAMAICA.

A congregation of free negroes in Jamaica adopted the following address to the family of the late Mr. Sturge :—

At a meeting of the church and congregations in Spanish Town and Sligoville, in the parishes of St. Catherine's and St. Thomas in the Vale, Jamaica, under the pastoral care of the Rev. J. M. Phillippo, it was unanimously resolved :—

" That this meeting has heard with deep sorrow of the death of their devoted friend and benefactor, Joseph Sturge, Esq., and hereby express their heart-felt sympathy with the friends of religion, of justice, and of humanity at large, in that affecting Providence by which they have been called to sustain the loss of so distinguished a Christian and philanthropist.

" They more especially express their condolence with Mrs. Sturge and family, who under such painful circumstances, in relation to the suddenness of the bereavement, mourn the loss of so affectionate and devoted a husband, father, and friend. But while they so deeply deplore his loss and record their testimony to the great and varied excellences of Mr. Sturge's character in the relationships both of public and private life, as connected more immediately with the interests of his native land, this meeting, consisting chiefly of emancipated peasantry, cannot but feel themselves laid under the deepest obligations on account of his long, arduous, and unwavering advocacy of their rights as men and as British subjects, particularly for his noble and generous conduct in personally visiting the West Indies in 1837, (well remembered by many of them), in order to acquaint himself with the odious system of apprenticeship to which they were then subject, and by which he was enabled to collect the facts that so effectually moved the people and Parliament of England to effect their complete emancipation.

" This boon, which it need scarcely be said they estimate beyond all price, and for which they trust they are increasingly thankful, they attribute chiefly under God, to the efforts of their departed friend and his associate, Thomas Harvey, Esq ; and they are persuaded that in this testimony they speak the sentiments of the whole emancipated population, not only of Jamaica, but those of the enfranchised people of all the British Colonies.

"All feel that they are bereaved of a friend and benefactor whose anxiety and efforts for their welfare have never been surpassed, and will ever associate the name of Sturge in their recollection with Clarkson, Wilberforce, Buxton, and others, gone also to their reward—the noblest and best friends of the African race that history records.

"Mr. Sturge, however, not only occupied the highest rank as an abolitionist; while he endeavoured to free the body of the slave from degrading vassalage, he, to the last hour of his life, consecrated his influence and property towards raising him, by Christian education, to that rank in the scale of being of which, by his circumstances and condition, he had been so unjustly deprived. But for his unfaltering generosity in this department of benevolence also (by no means the least important,) and that of others of the Society of Friends in particular, in aiding the various educational establishments in Jamaica, as many of this meeting can testify, few would have emerged from the abject mental condition in which the dark reign of slavery had left them.

"In recording their expressions of grief, in common with the whole of their brethren acquainted with Mr. Sturge's sympathies and efforts for the advancement of both their temporal and spiritual welfare, this meeting would not forget that the event was the result of His all-wise ordination, who doeth what pleaseth him in the armies of heaven and among the inhabitants of the earth.

"They would, therefore, humbly acquiesce in the dispensation, and adore the Divine goodness which supported their devoted friend through so long a period of usefulness, and enabled him to perform such a series of eminent services as distinguished his life; and earnestly pray that his children, and all who were privileged with his acquaintance, together with all who may hereafter know his worth, may imitate him in all that ennobled and distinguished him as a philanthropist, and in everything that was amiable and attractive in his character as a Christian."

The following will also prove that there is no exaggeration in this line of the Poem :—

"Grave senators forego debate."

" A meeting of the committee for providing some memorial to the late Joseph Sturge was held on Wednesday; Wm. Middle-more, Esq., in the chair. Letters were read from Lord Brougham, several distinguished members of Parliament, including Mr. Cobden and Mr. Bright, the Lord Mayor of London, and others, expressing their willinguess to co-operate in doing honour to Mr. Sturge's memory. It has been resolved to call a meeting of the committee on an early day to consider the character of the memorial, and organize the committee to carry out the decision that may be arrived at."

SECOND MEETING.

A general meeting of the committee and others favourable to the promotion of a memorial to the late Mr. Joseph Sturge, was held in the committee-room of the Town Hall, Birmingham, on Wednesday, to adopt the necessary measures to carry into effect such resolutions as might be determined upon. Sir John Ratcliff, mayor, was called upon to preside. Alderman Manton read communications from Mr. R. Cobden, M. P., and Mr. Bright, M. P.

The Mayor afterwards moved, "That this meeting acknow-ledging the claims of the late Mr. Sturge to the grateful recollec-tion of his fellow-countrymen, cordially approve of the proposal to raise a memorial of his eminent public virtues," which was seconded by the Rev. John Angell James, in an eloquent speech.

The resolution being carried, a committee, with Lord Brougham as chairman, was appointed, and it was determined that the funds raised should be applied, in the first instance, to the erection of a statue and fountain, and if possible, in further promoting some benevolent object in harmony with Mr. Sturge's character.

A Denominational periodical, THE PRIMITIVE CHURCH MAGAZINE, *of the Baptist School, had also the following notice on the decease of this eminent man.*

"MR. JOSEPH STURGE.—This eminent philanthropist died on Saturday, May 15, after but a few minutes' illness, in the sixty-sixth year of his age. Few men were more loved in life, or will be more missed in death. He was a true Christian cosmopolitan —a citizen of the world in a noble degree. His purse, his influence, and his large experience, were ever employed for the advancement of human welfare. He took a first rank among the friends of education, liberty, and peace. The cause of the Negro lay very near his heart, and to the emancipation and improvement of that oppressed race he devoted some of the best years of his life. His princely munificence scarcely knew anything of sectarian distinctions; and while his position and influence gave him a place among the first men of the land, he maintained the most unassuming simplicity and gentleness of character that could be well conceived. He has gone to his rest, and we are left to lament that so few remain to supply his place."

How truly the above testimonies to departed worth illustrate the truth of Holy Scripture, "THE MEMORY OF THE JUST IS BLESSED."

TO MR. J. A. JONES,

Pastor of the Baptist Church, Jireh Chapel, London, on completing the Fortieth year of his Pastorate, and the Fiftieth year of his public ministry.

———

Thou messenger of Truth Divine !
  Allow an *unknown* muse a line,*
    Thy patriarch age to cheer.
Hail to the man whose stedfast soul,
While changing seasons round him roll,
And mortals rove from pole to pole,
    Remains to Truth sincere.

Near four-score summer suns have shed
Their heat and toil upon thy head,
    To lay thee low and faint;
But He whose "standard" thou hast kept,
Both when a drowsy Church has slept,
Or thine own eye perchance has wept,—
    Has ne'er forsook his Saint.

From early youth to manhood's prime,
Through all thy sorrows,—all thy time,
    His love has been thy " rest ;"

———

* The writer remains to this day *personally* unknown to the above venerable minister.

And when the foe with threat'ning pride,
Has vow'd to make thy footsteps slide,
Thy Jesus stoop'd to be thy guide,
    And calm thy troubled breast.

Full oft thine ear has heard around,
The " trumpet" give " uncertain sound,"
    And spread a false belief ;
Full oft thine eye, o'er truth betray'd
By words polite,—or rudely made,
To serve some hireling " trick of trade,"—
    Has wept with silent grief.

But thou the path of " shining light"
Hast onward trod amid the night
    Of errors' treach'rous gloom ;
No " changeling" thou,—nor pelf, nor pay,
Could lure thy honest heart astray,
Or make thee " hireling of the day,"
    To meet a traitor's doom.

Thy " JIREH," long thine earthly home,
From whence nor foot nor thought could roam,
    To seek a broader fold ;
Has richly own'd thy fost'ring care,
And back repaid thy faith and prayer,
And all thy holy labours there,
    In tender accents told.

The fathers there "strong meat" have found,
And " new born babes" with "milk" abound,
　　Prepared by pious toil ;
" Deep things of God" have there found place ;—
The "secret of the Lord" and Grace,
Surpassing far all time and space,
　　Enrich the sacred soil.

The Pastor, distant type of him,
Whose strength ne'er fail'd, whose eye, ne'er dim,
　　Survey'd lov'd Canaan's shore ;
Looks onward to yon heav'nly clime,
And deems the day, the day of prime,
When he shall bid adieu to time,
　　And rise to sin no more.

But Father, ere the glorious day,
That bears thy faithful soul away,
　　Shall dawn in yonder skies,
Say,—when thy chariot we surround,
Shall there be some *Elisha* found,
To raise thy mantle from the ground,
　　And in thy stead arise ?

Till then, O stay, and fill thy place ;
Too few thy like,—too few with grace
　　Thy steady course to run ;

Vent not too soon, the strong desire
To mount the Car of heavenly fire,
Lest we should lose the noble Sire,
   Ere we secure the Son.

TO THE YEAR OF WAR, 1855.

"Watchman, what of the night?"

FAREWELL, Old Year, a long farewell,
Resistless fate has rung thy knell ;
And laid thee in the silent grave,
Where sleep both tyrant and his slave,
There rest thee in thy lonely cell,
Farewell Old Year, a long farewell !

Dark was the morning of thy birth,
With rolling clouds and gloom unbroken ;
   No sound was there but " War on Earth,"
By deep sepulchral voices spoken.
No Eastern Sages from afar,
Led by some radiant morning Star,
Beheld where lay the infant Stranger,
Sweet peace embodied in a manger.
No music of angelic strain,
Gladden'd the heart of shepherd swain ;

Or pour'd the dulcet sounds of love.
On man below, from God above ;
But demon furies gather'd there,
And call'd thee child of black despair.

Thy day advanc'd with noise and thunder,
Gloomy and dark with shades of night ;
The startled nations broke asunder,
To close again in deadly fight.
We heard the din of battle roar,
Upon the dread Crimean shore ;
We saw the torch and ghastly flame,
While shouting warriors call'd it "fame :"
But hope, that yet endeared deceiver,
That lures and mocks each true believer,
Protested that thy genial breath,
Would stay the flood and flame of death ;
And where the gory torrent ran,
Thy voice would speak " Good will to man."
But all in vain,—thy blind career,
Has prov'd a blank, thou dark Old Year ;
Nay, worse than blank,—thy deeds of crime,
Have backward turn'd " the course of time ;"
Check'd the precession of the spheres,
And spoil'd the work of peaceful years.
By thee restor'd, brute power alone,
Is made the guardian of the throne ;

And honour'd in the warlike deed,
Above the Monarch, law, and creed.
Thus hast thou turn'd the stream of life,
T , pools of blood,—thou year of strife,
And done thy wont to make thy page,
The Hist'ry of an " Iron age."

And shalt thou now escape the doom,
That truth pronounces o'er thy tomb?
Or the stern epitaph erase
Inscrib'd upon thy resting place ?
Ask yonder plains replete with beauty,
Where peace and virtue, love and duty,
Revell'd in rich and sweet abundance,
While joy flow'd on to full redundance :—
Ask why they mourn? Why now the weeping?
Why haggard childhood starts from sleeping,
And craves with wild and anxious eye,
The widow'd mother's scant supply ?
Why the bent form of woman there,
Is but the shadow of despair ?
Why she, who once with woman's pride,
Yielded to be a blushing bride ;
Pours maniac curses on the day,
That tore Heaven's choicest gift away,
Then stretch'd him 'midst the battle's roar,
A mangled corpse on foreign shore ;

And fix'd her fate, with infant band,
To be scorn'd paupers in the land ?
    O fatal year! Thy solemn doom
    Is writ in blood upon thy tomb!

    Or turn we to yon City proud,
Whose busy streets and countless crowd,
Proclaim afar the nation's glory,
Surpassing aught in ancient story.
Athens, beside her splendour, wanes,
And Rome bows lowly on her plains.
Golconda's famed or fabled mines,
Grow dim where Britain's Babel shines.
And he, the King and Seer of old,
Who sat and stood on burnish'd gold,
Whose pomp and wisdom spread the fame
And greatness of the monarch's name ;
Moving a mighty Queen to own,
The untold splendours of his throne ;
—" In all his glory" saw no power,
From Judah's height or Salem's tower,
So great in wealth, so nobly blest,
As the new mistress of the West.
    But thou vile year of war and woe,
Hast bent her neck and brought her low ;
Her magnates blinding by thy power,
To yield her wealth and raise thy dower.

For thee, thou Monster of the night,
They love the darkness more than light,
" Resolving," with befitting looks,
To pay for bullets,—not for books.
For thee they vow by open deed,
That mind may starve, but war must feed ;
That Science is an empty bubble,
In days when " Income Tax" is double.
Charm'd by thy glance they nobly spare,
When bloodshed stands the suppliant there ;
But when meek knowledge begs a ray,
Of sacred light to cheer the day,
Abash'd, they drive her from the hall,
And show how States begin their fall.*

Thou dark Old year, are these thy deeds?
Is it by thee Creation bleeds?
Is it by thee the widow's woe
And orphans' tears are made to flow?

---

* " At a recent meeting of the Citizens of London, under the presidency of the Lord Mayor, to consider as to the application of the Public Library act, Mr. Ewart, M. P., proposed a resolution for the application of the act, which was seconded by Colonel Sykes, who showed the advantages enjoyed by other capitals over London in this matter. An amendment was moved by Mr. Deputy Peacock, and supported by Mr. Alderman Sydney and others, that a public library was unnecessary in the present state of taxation. *The amendment was carried by a large majority.*"

H

It is by thee great London feels,
The tread of want upon her heels ;
And deems it no dishonour's mark
To keep her people in the dark ?
Go then—receive thy final doom,
And hide thy guilt within the tomb.
Go, and beneath yon kindred yew,
Entomb thy Moloch spirit too.
Around that spot by ev'ry tongue
Thy joyful requiem shall be sung ;
While the glad news o'er earth shall spread,
" *The troubler of the world is dead.*"

"A HAPPY NEW YEAR."

ADDRESSED TO THE YEAR 1858.

"Blessed are the Peacemakers."

HAIL to thee, Stranger, first-born of the morning,
Quiet and sweet thou breathest o'er our earth ;
Hail to thy smile the rosy East adorning,
Though Winter reigns triumphant at thy birth.

Thou comest fresh from spheres with joy redundant,
Where the young minutes play around Old Time,

Where bright-robed Venus sheds her light abundant,
And glory rolls in symphony sublime.

But say, thou offspring of departed ages,
Thou smiling infant of yon heavenly sphere ;
Say, (for no voice escapes our dumb-struck Sages,)
Say, what thy message, what thy errand here ?

Art thou come charged our land and world to gladden,
Singing anew of heavenly "Peace on Earth ?"
Or art thou ministrant of woe, to sadden,
By mingling carnage with our cup of mirth ?

Art thou the Herald of a fairer mission,
Than thy departed Sisters were of late ?   [contrition
Who breathed forth war, and mock'd, when meek
Call'd for a tear on deeds of blood and hate ?

Who more need Peace than we of Christian calling ?
Who more than we are deeply stained with blood ?
Our martial " glory" thrives by deeds appalling,
And fame lies through of human gore, a flood.

See yonder hills that skirt the *Euxine* waters,
Or distant Persia with her solemn plains ;
Or where dull China stunts her growing daughters,
Or the dark Indian dozes o'er his pains :—

The Crimean hill, the Persian plain and city,
The Chinese widow and the Indian rude ;
Alike proclaim the Saxon void of pity,
When lust of Empire prompts to deeds of blood.

And where his right ? Or where the compensation,
So loudly boasted by the Saxon proud ?
Where liberty ? Or where the ' upraised' nation ?
Or freedom given to a fettered crowd ?

Where has the Soldier spread the people's banner,
And by his sword sent forth the captive free ?
Have Poland's plains, or Indian savannah,
Received the boon of British liberty ?

On what dark shore,—within what Despot's border,
Has *he* made thought, *free thought*, the sovereign rule ?
Where has *he* fixed opinion, law, and order,
In lieu of fetters, and the tyrant's school ?

What Senate free,—what state controlled by reason,
Has Saxon *bloodshed* started into life ?
When has the world known less of crime or "treason,"
By all his carnage, all his savage strife ?

No.—The bold soldier,—dauntless in his error,
Brave in a cause he vainly deems the right ;

Knows not that virtue nothing owes to terror,
That freedom perishes where nations fight.*

And yet I love thee, Britain,—first of nations ;
Land of my fathers, and my natal home ;
From thy sweet shores through distant generations,
We ne'er have wander'd, ne'er have wished to roam.

Yet Fatherland, I cannot love or cherish,
Thy sins of blood-shed, or thy conq'ring pride ;
Long live thy greatness,—never may it perish,
May thy TRUE GLORY evermore abide.

But is that "glory" which through generations,
Has reared the robber,† and produced the brute ?‡

---

* "War, very far from being the progress of humanity, is only murder in mass, which retards it, afflicts it, decimates it, dishonours it. The nations who sport in blood, are instruments of ruin, not instruments of life, to the world. They may grow, but they grow contrary to the purpose of God, and end by losing in one day of justice, that which they have conquered through years of violence."—*Lamartine.*

† "The wealth of Clive was such as enabled him to vie with the first grandees of England. There remains proof that he had remitted more than a hundred and eighty thousand pounds through the Dutch East Indian Company, and more than forty thousand pounds through the English Company. The amount which he had sent home through private houses was also considerable. His purchase of diamonds, at Madras alone, amounted to twenty-five thousand pounds. Besides a great mass of ready money, he had his Indian estate, valued by himself at twenty-

Which round the earth has spread dark desolations,
Its spirit murder, and all crime its fruit ?*

Is it true "glory" to expend huge treasure,
On distant conquest, when thy poor want bread?
From labour's brow to drive each trace of pleasure,
That men of blood with plenty may be fed?

Or is it " glory" to a noble nation,
To carry "DEBT" for ever on its name ?

---

seven thousand a year.—We may safely affirm that no Englishman who started with nothing has ever, in any line of life,
created such a fortune *at the early age of thirty-four.*"—*Lord
Macauley's Essay on Lord Clive.*

‡ It should not be forgotten that the "Sepoy" class, recently
so notorious for cruelty, were under our training for 100 years
or more. What that training has made or left them, let the
late "atrocities" declare.

* "War is the fruitful parent of crimes. It reverses, with
respect to its objects, all the rules of morality. It is nothing
less than a temporary repeal of the principles of virtue. It is
a system out of which almost all the virtues are excluded, and
in which nearly all the vices are included."— *Robert Hall.*

"*Thus was the city won, and then did the British Soldiers who
had crossed the seas to rescue Spaniards from French thraldom,
rush upon the city, and slaughter, and pillage, and violate every
house. There was no order, no restraint; officers were shot in the
streets by drunken soldiers; old men and women they slaughtered
promiscuously;.........whole families were burnt up in their own
houses; and thus reigned horror and dreadful carnage for several
days in succession. The after-scene was indeed 'hell broke loose.'*"
—*Col. Napier on the Storming of Badajoz.*

To stand forth branded through the wide creation,
With spendthrift folly, or a pauper's fame ?*

Truth, mercy, justice,—these *alone* are " glory,"
And these nor ask, nor take the aid of sots ;†

---

* Of every pound paid by the English people in their taxation, more than 17s. 6d. is swallowed up by war and war forces, and less than 2s. 6d. spent upon civil government. The amount lavished on Warlike establishments and their liabilities *during the present century alone* is not less than THREE THOUSAND MILLIONS sterling ! Is it surprising that numbers among the population often find it difficult to obtain an honest living? The bare *interest* alone of the National Debt since 1815 has exceeded *One Thousand Millions* sterling ! How far posterity may acknowledge the obligations of a debt which they never contracted remains to be proved ; but it would involve a fearful hazard to the State should they ever agitate the *morality* of the claim.

† Is the term too strong for many of the men on whom is devolved the work of our national " glory ?"—Let the following account from Burnley answer the question. " Between eight and nine o'clock on New Year's Eve, a number of the men belonging to the 100th Dublin Militia, now lying in the Burnley barracks, commenced a disturbance in the town. Most of them were in a state of intoxication, and when they turned into the streets they became violent, attacking indiscriminately all who came within their reach." The conduct of the militia is described as perfectly wild ; they howled, struck their bayonets in the causeway, and one of them sharpened his bayonet on a door step, calling to his comrades to do the same, and give it to the English.

" The sights I saw, both going and returning [on Sunday]

Nor need they cruel warfare, nor the story,
Of weeping widows, and of blazing cots.

Time was when wisdom, lordly in her station,
Gave to " opinion" all the power and fame ;
But wisdom died, and " glory" fled the nation,
Leaving to folly but her empty name.*

And has not folly, has not dark illusion,
Imposed full oft on patriots and on peers,—
Have not base hirelings, trading in delusion,
Raised goblin shadows to provoke our fears ?

Is it that truth, if honestly outspoken,
Too soon would show our "glory" but a curse ?
Or lay too bare how streams of wealth unbroken
Enrich but paupers on the public purse ?

---

were enough to make an Englishman despair of his countrymen.
All along the road were men—not only privates, but non-com-
missioned officers—in every stage of drunkenness. Sobriety was
really the exception, intoxication the rule."—*The Crimean
Correspondent of the Times, October* 22nd, 1854.

* " It is quite true it may be said, what are opinions against
armies ? SIR, MY ANSWER IS, OPINIONS ARE STRONGER THAN
ARMIES. OPINIONS, IF THEY ARE FOUNDED IN TRUTH AND JUSTICE,
WILL, IN THE END, PREVAIL AGAINST THE BAYONETS OF INFANTRY,
THE FIRE OF ARTILLERY, AND THE CHARGES OF CAVALRY."—*Lord
Palmerston, in* 1849.

Or is it meant, that lured by distant battle,
Britons may mock at sterner claims at home ?
So the fond babe amused with gilded rattle,
Permits the nurse among coquets to roam.*

Alas for England! Philistines have bound her,
While, Samson-like, she sleeps on danger's arm ;
Oh that her sons would quickly gather round her,
To burst her fetters, and dissolve the charm!

Thou Stranger year, thou first-born of the morning,
Awake my lov'd, my native land from sleep ;
If long delayed, too late will come the warning,
Too late when doom'd, *as we have sown, to reap.*

A New Year happy be thou lovely Stranger,
Bring to our world sweet mercy, truth, and peace;

---

* In years of peace we obtained the repeal of the Test and
Coporation Acts—Catholic and Negro Emancipation—the
Reform Bill—Free Trade—the Penny Postage—Corporation
Reform—Reform of the Tariff—Popular Education—Cheap
Newspapers—Railways—the Electric Telegraph, &c., &c. But
when the Russian war began every reform was suspended—
home affairs sunk into a condition of utter neglect, and the
people were "amused" with battles and bombardments *a long
way off*, as a compensation for the postponement of all progress
among themselves. If, however, the people allow distant wars
to be their " gilded rattle," while taxes are heaped upon taxes,
until gaunt poverty shall look them more fully than ever in the
face, *the blame will lie at their own door alone.*

Renew the strain, as when o'er Bethl'm's manger,
Angelic voices bade all discord cease.

Drive to their dens the malice-breathing legions,
Who prompt mankind to shed each other's gore;
And loud proclaim through earth's afflicted regions,
That War and bloodshed shall afflict no more.

SAMUEL'S PRAYER. (1 Samuel iii. 9, 10).

(Written for a Child).

"Speak, Lord, thy servant heareth,"
    I'll listen to thy voice;
My heart within me feareth,—
    O make that heart rejoice!

For I have oft mistaken
    Thy voice for one below;
Yet leave me not forsaken,
    To perish in my woe.

"Speak, Lord," in lovingkindness;
    Thy voice is sweet and mild;
Forgive my sinful blindness,
    Since I am but a child.

And I will love thee ever,
  As grace shall fill my heart,
And from thy service never,—
  No, NEVER, NEVER PART.

JUBILEE CHORUS.

(TO "MIRIAM'S SONG.")

*Written for the celebration of the Fiftieth Anniversary of the
pastorate over the same people of a venerable Baptist
Minister.*

RAISE the loud chorus, now raise it on high,
  Our Jesus has conquer'd and reigns in the sky!
Sing, for the gates of the tomb are now broken,
  By him who is mighty to pardon and save;
In vain Hell resisted, for Jesus hath spoken,
  And scattered the forces of death and the grave.
Raise the loud chorus, now raise it on high,
Our Jesus has conquer'd and reigns in the sky!

Raise the loud chorus, now raise it on high,
Our Jesus has conquer'd and reigns in the sky!
Sing for the honours, O saints, that await you,
  When high in his kingdom his glory you see;
When he shall have blasted the foes that now hate you,
  And called you to join in the Great Jubilee.
Raise the loud chorus, &c.

Raise the loud chorus, now raise it on high,
Our Jesus hath conquer'd and reigns in the sky!
Sing, for each year brings us nearer that gladness,
    When pastor and people shall meet round the throne,
And shout the farewell to all sorrow and sadness,
    And welcome the glories to mortals unknown.
Raise the loud chorus, now raise it on high,
AND LET IT RESOUND THROUGH THE EARTH AND THE
SKY.

Postscript.

A PERMANENT CONGRESS OF EUROPEAN NATIONS AS A SUBSTITUTE FOR WAR.

SUCH a congress is *possible.* If a congress can be held to settle a dispute *after* war, surely there is nothing impossible in forming one *before* war has been resorted to at all. It is a pure absurdity to contend that rational human beings (and all *nations* are rational) require bloodshed as indispensable to the exercise of reason. Such an argument would disgrace even the brute creation.

We have in Europe the Cowleys, the Clarendons, and the Russels,—the Walewskies, and the Lamartines,—the Cavours, —the Bunsens,—the Mantueffels,—the Orloffs, and other men eminent for political knowledge, and well versed in the true economy of states, on whom might be devolved the important duty of inaugurating such a congress. As eminent for patriotism as for diplomatic skill, they would be among the last to sacrifice their country's honour at the shrine of a feeble expediency ; yet, fully aware of the nature and calamities of war, they would be found among the first to confess that the decision of the sword is always uncertain,—that victory as often remains with the wrong party as with the right,—that war is, at the best, but a trial of strength and not of reason,—and that the honour derived from the pugilism of the battle-field is a degradation and a disgrace to rational man.

When, above two centuries since, Henry IV., of France, propounded his celebrated scheme for a permanent confederacy of the European nations in order to prevent war, it was never pleaded that such an object was *impossible.* Has Europe, then, so far degenerated, or so little improved, during more than two hundred years, that what was possible then is impossible now ? If such be the case, let us hide our diminutive stature from the shades of our ancestors, or they will break the silence of the tomb in expressions of shame upon their dwarfish sons. In the noble plan of Henry, he assigned to France, Spain, Great Britain, Denmark, Sweden, Lombardy, Germany, the Papacy, Poland and Venice, four representatives each. To Hungary, Bohemia, Italy, Switzerland and Belgium, two representatives each. Russia and Turkey were not prominent at that period among the European, states. The members were to have been appointed by their respective governments once in three years. The states general of the United Provinces, the Landgrave of Hesse, the Prince of Anhalt, the Protestants of Hungary, Bohemia, and Lower Austria, several of the princes and towns of Germany, most of the Swiss cantons, and our own Queen Elizabeth, promptly concurred in the proposal, and were arranging to be represented in the council, when the dagger of the assassin laid prostrate the royal author amidst the lamentations of a disappointed continent.

The Council of Amphictyon, the Lycian Confederacy, the Achean League, the Helvetic Union, and a number of other confederacies, prove the *possibility* of a congress on a larger scale. There is nothing wanted but that some one of the great European states should be bold enough to make the proposal, as Henry IV. had the moral courage to do, and our groaning humanity would respond to the call with an echo of universal joy. O that England,—my beloved England,—my home, my fatherland,—would repeat her own noble example ! She was the first among the nations to break the fetters of the slave, and the world has rewarded her with its highest honour. Would that she were also the first to emancipate the citizen from the despotism of the sword ! A more than double honour would crown the deed, and unborn generations would bless her memory.

BRISCOE, Printer, Banner Street, Finsbury.

APPENDIX.

Contents :

APPENDIX.

"THY WILL BE DONE."

WHEN bereft of every joy,
    When dark cares my thoughts employ,
When fierce enemies annoy,
            Thy will be done.

When the heart is filled with fear,
When the eye pours sorrow's tear,
When foreboding ills are near,
            Thy will be done

When each pleasing scene has fled,
When fond hope itself is dead,
When all skies are overspread,
            Thy will be done.

When the tempter's power is nigh,
When the tempest rages high,
When loud thunders shake the sky,
            Thy will be done.

When the last great foe shall bring,
Mortal terror in his sting,
Then I'll lift my voice and sing,
            Thy will be done.

When around this earthly ball,
Death shall cast the fun'ral pall,
Then in nobler worlds—by all,
    Thy will be done.

THE SAINT'S FAREWELL.

Written on the Death of the late Miss ORMEROD, who, for thirty-seven years was a most useful member of the Strict Baptist Church, formerly at Irwell-terrace, and recently at Zion Chapel, Bacup. Her unostentatious piety and unassuming manners, endeared her to a large circle of religious persons of various denominations—while her unchanging attachment to the Strict Baptist cause, afforded an example of unflinching adherence to simple New Testament truth, worthy of a close and persevering imitation. "She being dead, yet speaketh."

FAREWELL! ye scenes of pain and strife,—
  Ye friendships of this lower life—
    A long, a last farewell!
I hear a voice that bids me rise,
And wing my way to yonder skies,
    Where perfect spirits dwell.

My "earthly house," my mortal home,
No more confined in thee to roam;
    I lay thee down to die.
Come Death, and make this frame thy prey,
'Tis all thou dar'st to take away;
    'Tis thy sole victory.

Yet, Monster, know that He who died
On Calvary— the Crucified—
 Gives thee that frame in trust.
Go—hide it in thy thickest gloom—
Secrete it in thy deepest tomb—
 And mix it with the dust.

Once more He'll pierce thy dark domain,
And call that dust to life again,
 And be its living Head.
He'll speak, and thou, O Death, shalt die,
While Heav'n shall echo " VICTORY !
 DEATH—DEATH ITSELF IS DEAD !"

Then do thy bidding, Death ;—to me
Thy stroke is life, and liberty ;
 And everlasting gain !
With joy I part from things below
To soar above this vale of woe ;
 This land of sin and pain.

Adieu ! ye saints of God on earth—
Ye children of the second birth,
 Endeared by sacred ties ;
Long have I shared your joy and fear,
But now I leave my " Zion" here,
 For Zion in the skies.

Pilgrims for heaven, be strong, be bold;
On God and truth seize firm your hold;
   Be faithful, and adore.
Time swiftly flies,—soon all shall meet,
To worship at Immanuel's feet,
   And cry " Farewell " no more.

LINES ON THE DEATH OF PRINCE ALBERT.

SILENCE, ye nations!—earth, adore!
  And bend, ye monarchs!—bend before
   The hand that wields the rod.*
The gentle Albert sleeps in death;
Hushed be each tongue—subdued each breath,
While rolls th' Almighty voice, and saith,
   " Be still,—and own your God."

You palaced home is dark with grief,
And royal hearts but find relief,
   In Israel's God and King.
Alas! How vain is splendour now,
The glittering throng, the studied bow,
When sorrow clouds each noble brow,
   And courts with anguish ring!

---

* Micah vi. 9.

Oh, Death! must thou another dart,
Hurl at the tender, weeping heart,
   Of her whose griefs we share?
Were there no humbler victims nigh,
But thou a *second* shaft must fly,
And fix with cruel hand on high,
   Another arrow there?†

Remorseless Death! Unfeeling foe!
Why blindly deal a double blow,
   And double sorrows trace?
Mercy adorns the nobly brave,
But thou, and thy compeer, the grave,
No mercy show to king, or slave,
   To country, clime, or race.

O Death! the present is thine hour,
And thou hast pluck'd a princely flower,
   Forth from the Royal stem.
We mourn our loss,—we mourn the blank,
That thou hast made in noble rank;—
We mourn the day when Albert sank,
   Like some bright ocean gem.

Britain! let fall the genial tear;
Thy throne is sad, thy palace drear,
   And joy forsakes the scene.

---

† The Duchess of Kent died on the 16th March, 1861.

In all that grief bear thy full part;
A double woe, a double dart,
Have pierced that Queenly, widowed heart;
THEN PRAY FOR ENGLAND'S QUEEN!

THE CHRISTIAN'S BATTLE SONG.

ARM Warriors, arm; the foe is strong,
The battle fierce, the conflict long;
The Prince of Hell, with frowning might,
Aloud defies you to the fight.
Arm Warriors, arm; hurl back defiance,
On heaven's sure word place firm reliance.

Arm Warriors, arm; awake be bold,
The lion prowls about the fold;
Awake! or while you idly sleep,
The foe breaks in upon the sheep.
Arm Warriors, arm; shout "No surrender!
The Lord of Hosts is our Defender."

Arm Warriors, arm; a fiery dart,
Is aim'd at every warrior's heart;
Uplift the shield and rest no more,
Until the raging fight be o'er.
Arm Warriors, arm; unfurl the banner,
And raise the battle cry, "Hosanna."

Arm Warriors, arm ; the crafty foe,
Lurks but to deal a secret blow ;
Gird on the sword, and in its might,
Go forth and put the foe to flight.
Arm Warriors, arm ; the great deceiver,
Shall fly before each weak believer.*

Arm Warriors, arm ; your Captain calls,
And bids you watch upon the walls ;†
His matchless power and wakeful eye,
Shall guard where thickest arrows fly ;
Then Warriors, arm ; be firm and steady,
And at your Captain's call stand ready.

Arm Warriors, arm ; a noble prize,
Awaits each conq'ror in the skies ;
There all who fought and stood their ground,
Are with immortal honour crown'd.
Then Warriors, arm ; a prize all glorious,
Awaits the brow of the victorious.‡

MATLOCK-BATH.

ᴸ ᴇᴛ Fashion take her wayward flight,
To every distant Alpine height ;
Let pamper'd "cits" and country " swells,"
Run wild in search of fairer dells ;

---

* Eph. vi. 10—20.   † Isa. lxii. 6 ; Ezek. xxxiii. 6, 7.
‡ Rev. ii. 10 ; iii. 21.

Let town-made "taste," and rustic lore,
Rush breathless to some foreign shore,
And twist their Saxon to the cry,
That "Britain knows no 'classic' sky."

To me no foreign dell or strand,
Is lovely as my native land.
No Alpine height with "cloud-capp'd tower,"
Whose pride defies the thunder's power;
No Tempé, with *Olympus* high,
Or Naples and her azure sky;
Can charm the heart with scenes so sweet,
As round this noble Matlock meet.

O boasting Rhine! I've traced thy stream
To learn how soon grave scholars dream;
With fond admiring eye have hung,
On all that German poets sung;
And paid the tribute, warm and true,
To nature's beauties ever due.
But not thy boldest scene, O Rhine!
Can vie with this sweet land of mine.

Thy *Drachenfels*, and seven-fold peaks,
Whose crags the lonely eagle seeks;
Thy *Roland* and his mythic maid,
In midway stream for ever laid;
Thy scattered ruins, black and bare,
Prints of a race no longer there;

Though deck'd in richest garb,—they stand,
Far shaded by this fairy land.*

Here nature in her loveliest mood,
Spreads all her beauty to the flood ;
Tempting her swain with sylvan song,
His love-lorn visits to prolong.
Her Derwent hears the vocal strain,
Responsive on the glowing plain,
And tarries where, with brightest charms,
His nymph invites with open arms.

O Rhine! no love like this is found,
On Grecian or on German ground.
Thy mountains groan,—thy rocks complain
Of solitude,—but all in vain.
And all in vain thy relics spread,
O'er every haggard mountain head ;
On no proud height such beauties meet,
As gather round Victoria's feet.†

---

* "—— to a traveller who has seen most of the Scottish highlands, there is a tameness and a sameness in the scenery of the Rhine, which soon palls the taste.—Above all, everything is too near. It wants distance to give enchantment to the view." —*Eight Weeks in Germany, p.* 114.

† "Victoria stand;" a tower erected on "*the heights of Abraham*," Matlock Bath, in 1844, to commemorate the visit of Her Majesty to that delightful spot, when Princess Victoria. From that elevated "stand," and especially from the Masson point above, or the "Black Rocks" across the valley to the south-west, one of the sweetest, and most sublime prospects in Europe may be surveyed.

Great England's Queen, Victoria—Hail!
Thy smile yet cheers this lovely dale;
And in yon bold, majestic tower,
We see an emblem of thy power.
We ask no castellated walls,
With spear, and lance, and blood-stained halls,
Or frowning fort* from yonder Rhine,
To guard that hallowed throne of thine.

We would not mar these matchless heights,
With ruins of old feudal fights,
Whence foemen proud—*too proud to feel*—
Went forth to battle, or to steal.
Warm, loving hearts, more nobly brave,
Than courage round the warrior's grave;
These, these, O Queen, these we resign,
To guard that sacred throne of thine.

Not from the past, the feudal age,
With bloodshed on each rolling page;
Not from the deeds of ancient strife,
May we draw hope of better life.
Forward,—the past is writ in woe,
When man but lived to man a foe;
Forward,—true glory lies before,
Where wiser men "learn war no more."†

* Ehrenbreitstein.
† Isa. ii. 4. Surely it is more ennobling to look forward to
the glorious future, than to be perpetually travelling back to the
exploded maxims of the past! Surely a barbaric feudalism is
not to supply us with mischievous playthings *for ever!*

O Matlock! may thy scenes inspire,
This onward zeal, this purer fire.
May Derwent, as his waters roll,
But image peace from pole to pole :—
And O may yonder shaded grove,
The fond retreat and "walk" of love,*
Be but the type of coming mind,
When love, not war, shall rule mankind.

Thou King of kings,—thou God of love,
Breathe thy pure Spirit from above;
The demon war, our world's great foe,
Hurl to his cavern'd home below.
Why should our earth for ever be,
A contrast dark to Heaven and Thee?
Why not, like smiling Matlock, rise,
And be another Paradise?

Hope Cottage, Matlock Bath,
 August, 1861.

TRUE MANHOOD.

Not he who rollicks in the gilded car,
 With gold-bespangled menials in his train,
And prancing steeds clanking the horseman's chain;
 Nor he who vaunts the "garter" and the "star,"

---

* The "Lover's Walk," a retreat of exquisite rural beauty, on the right bank of the Derwent, at Matlock Bath.

Whose roll ancestral travels back afar
Into dim darkness or the mist of ages,
Baffling the skill of grave and learned sages
To read aright the record of its pages,
And say who his first father—what his name—
Whether of tainted or untainted fame,
Or if of " gentle " blood or coarse he came ;
Not he whose honour rises in the dark,
Is the true man, or wears true manhood's mark.

Not he who revels in the transient smile
Of courts and nobles, and the circle gay
Of titled drones, who heartless honours pay
At foot of Royalty, and there beguile
Life's precious hours with mimic pomp and style,
Content with fashion's empty round of pleasure,
Or vain display of large but ill-spent treasure,
Bestowed on pride without or stint or measure,
While the poor ploughman labours on in grief,
And widowed hearts and orphans ask relief,
But bootless ask, where fashion reigns the chief;
Not he who thus his life to glitter gives
Is the true man, nor manhood in him lives.

But he true manhood knows, and only he,
Who drops a tear and bears a pang for all
Of humankind ; who, ready at the call
Of groaning suff'rer struggling to be free,

Will dauntless plead for golden liberty,
And, true to man, " in season, out of season,"
Will dare denounce, as black and deadly treason
To man's humanity, what clouds pure reason,
Or conscience checks, or throws a tyrant's chain
Around free thought, for lucre or for gain,
That despots may the more securely reign.
He who thus nobly treads life's narrow span,
Shows the TRUE MANHOOD in himself as man.

THE MARRIAGE OF THE PRINCE OF WALES.
SONG FOR THE BRIDAL DAY.

UPLIFT the broad banner, ye Saxons and Danes,
    And wide let it float over mountains and plains ;
A Prince among Nobles, a Dane in her beauty,
Unite in affection, in honour, and duty.

No Horsa, no Hengist, no Guthrun, or Sweyne,
Comes arm'd to subdue the first son of the Queen ;
No wild roving chieftain in battle-deeds hoary,
Advances, Old England to rob of its glory.

But still the Dane comes with all maidenly grace,
To conquer and capture the Prince of his race.
Awake, sons of Albion,—All England rejoices,
And hails Alexandra with jubilant voices.

A crown in the distance awaits but their day,
Yet may its assumption be far, far away;
A lov'd Queen adorns it,—still queenly in sadness,
But long may this day yield her solace and gladness.

Hail, Albert, and hail to the Star at thy side,
Be Heaven's best blessings on bridegroom and bride :
May loving affection that time cannot sever,
Blend both in one union for ever and ever.

As Prince, or as Monarch, may peace be thy stay,
Nor war, with its crimes, ever darken thy day;
Lead on, noble Albert, a new generation,
Till nation no more lift up sword against nation.

A gentleman in Lancashire having (quite unknown to the author) sent copies of the above song direct to the Prince of Wales, accompanied by a private letter,— his Royal Highness instructed his Secretary to forward the following reply. It is inserted here on account of the unaffected sympathy which it evinces towards the suffering operatives, by the heir-apparent to the British throne.

" *Buckingham Palace, March* 23, 1863.

"Sir,

"I am commanded by the Prince of Wales to thank you very much for the Hymn which you have been good enough to send him, and for the kind wishes which accompany it.

" His Royal Highness desires me further to say that he feels deeply sensible of the sentiments which his marriage has called forth in all parts of England; and to express his sorrow that in the manufacturing districts of the North of England, this occasion of rejoicing had of necessity so much to sadden it. I have the honour to be, Sir, your most obedient servant,

"HERBERT FISHER, *Private Secretary.*"

THE GLORIOUS FUTURE.

"Glorious things are spoken of thee, O city of God :"
Psa. lxxxvii. 3.

Lo ! from every distant mountain,
   Rank on rank from every plain ;
Devotees from Ganges' fountain,
   Captives freed from error's chain ;
     All are coming,
   Princes with their gorgeous train.*

Hark ! the chorus now ascending,
   Bears aloft the Saviour's name ;
Voices strong and strange are blending,
   In the great Messiah's fame ;
     And his glory,
   Round the universe proclaim.†

Angel hosts with joy adore him,
   Seated on th' eternal throne ;
Bending low, they sing before him,
   " Christ the Lamb is Lord alone."
     Earth and heaven,
   Him the great Redeemer own."‡

---

* Isa. xliii. 6 ; lx. 3.   † Isa. xlix. 13 ; li. 11.
‡ Heb. i. 6 ; Rev. v. 13.

Indian tribes no longer cherish,
Juggernaut and all his host;
Idols, at His bidding, perish,
From each distant sea-girt coast.
Christ the Saviour,
Now is ev'ry nation's boast.*

Slaves start forth with joyful voices,
Singing with a holy glee ;
Dark-skinned Africa rejoices,
In the word that speaks them free.
Through creation,
Sounds the hymn of liberty.†

War no longer with its thunder,
Fills the smiling plain with dread;
Blood no more shall drive asunder
Nations, to deplore their dead.
Heroes perish,
Where the Saviour deigns to tread.‡

Hasten on, great day of glory,
Hasten, blessed Jubilee !
Spread abroad the wondrous story,
Of the love on Calvary ;
Till all nations,
Shall its joy and triumph see.§

* Isa. ii. 18—21.   † Psa. lxxii. 4, 12—14.
‡ Psa. lxxii. 7 ; Isa. ii. 4 ; John xviii. 36.
§ Isa. lx. 6, 7, 12.

THE SOLDIER'S WIDOW.

SHE wept—and heavy were the tears,
 That marr'd her care-worn face ;
For smiles had long since fled,—and years
 Of grief, had seized their place.

Nor was there near some friendly hand,
 To wipe those tears away ;
For all alone on foreign strand,
 Her only comfort lay.

He, fair of form, her beauteous boy,
 Her treasure and her pride ;
Had grown to be the widow's joy,
 Close at the widow's side.

As ivy round some stately oak,
 So round her heart he twined ;
And when the tie that bound them, broke,
 It left no tie behind.

But all around a desert seems,
 Her home all blank and bare ;
Her lovely boy is in her dreams,
 Alas ! he's only there.

" Woe, woe the day," the widow cried,
 " Ah ! woe the doleful day ;
When he forsook his mother's side,
 To join in foreign fray.

" On yonder shore, where vultures start,
　　His father's blood they shed ;
And he who gained my youthful heart,
　　There fell among the dead.

　No tender wife was at his side,
　　His dying grief to share ;
O cruel fate ! alone he died ;
　　Alone he perished there !

" Nor have long rolling years erased,
　　From my fond heart, that pain ;
Yet in my boy I daily traced,
　　The father o'er again.

" And as he grew I loved to teach,
　　Of him whose name he bore ;
And oft he'd ask in simple speech,
　　' Will father come no more ?'

" But now no more, no never more,
　　May I the father trace ;
Nor in the form or name he bore,
　　Nor in that lovely face.

" O cruel War ! of man the foe,
　　Of foulest fiend the breath ;
Thy fond delights are in our woe,
　　Thy glory—in our death.

" O happy they to whom is given,
    To tear thy mask away ;
To show thy birth from hell, not heaven,
    And innocence thy prey.

" A Widow's curse be on thy head,
    Thou false and wicked one ;
For thou hast plung'd among thy dead,
    A Husband and a Son."

The Widow ceased ;—a solemn awe,
    O'er all her features spread ;
I look'd again, then, startled, saw,
    The Soldier's Widow,—DEAD.

"MY GOD."

"O God, thou art my God :" Psa. lxiii. 1.

MY God ! and may I ever claim,
    To know thee by that sacred name ?
Dearer that name, than all the gold,
That worldlings seek, and misers hold.

Art thou my God ?—my treasure fair ?
Art thou my glory and my care ?
Is this my chief delight to be,
Em tied of earth, and full of thee ?

Yes,—I no other care bestow,
On all that asks my care below;
All else is vain, an empty breath,
A shadow passing on to death.

Thou, Thou alone, art all in all,
And while before thy feet I fall,
My aching heart heaves forth the groan,
To be the shrine of God alone.

This, this is heaven to me below,
Thee as my Father God to know;
And my full joy in worlds above,
Will be to bear this seal of love.

Then Father, let my fleeting days
Be all devoted to thy praise;
And as my moments swiftly run,
Be this my theme, " Thy will be done."

ASCRIPTION.

Jehovah,—Three-in-One,
    Of sovereign love the Spring,
Thy will on earth be done,
    By peasant, priest, and king.
Before thy sacred feet we fall,
Great God of glory—All in all.

BRISCOE, Printer, Banner Street, Finsbury.

www.ingramcontent.com/pod-product-compliance
Lightning Source LLC
Chambersburg PA
CBHW031123020726
47495CB00007B/2324